THE
Last Mall Rat

THE
Last Mall Rat

Erik E. Esckilsen

Houghton Mifflin Company Boston 2003

Walter Lorraine Books

Walter Lorraine (wl) Books

Library of Congress Cataloging-in-Publication Data

Esckilsen, Erik.
  The last mall rat / by Erik E. Esckilsen.
      p. cm.
Summary: Too young to get a job at the Onion River Mall,
fifteen-year-old Mitch takes money from salesclerks to harass rude
shoppers.
  ISBN 0-618-23417-9
  [1. Shopping malls—Fiction.] I. Title.
  PZ7.E7447 Las 2003
  [Fic]—dc21

                                                    2002014436

Printed in the United States of America
QUM 10 9 8 7 6 5 4 3 2 1

For my mother, Joan

Acknowledgments

Special thanks for timely encouragement go to Megan Pels Carney and her former students at Rowland Hall St. Marks in Salt Lake City, Utah, and also to David C. Englander and his former students at John Stark Regional High School in Weare, New Hampshire. Old friend, writer, and teacher Tom French and teen super-reader Alana Miller offered constructive criticism just when I needed it most. Literary agent Wendy Schmalz's keen eye and instincts shaped this story in crucial ways—and she never gave up on it—for which I am indebted both to her and to Megan Tingley for introducing us (and for thinking a book might come of it). Finally, I thank Walter Lorraine for his courage in gambling on a newcomer and for excellent editorial guidance.

What living and buried speech is always vibrating here . . . what howls restrained by decorum.

—Walt Whitman, *Song of Myself*

Under the Table

1

As I step out of ShUSA and into the mall, my Chuck Taylors make a piercing squeak on the tiles. The sound is like a match striking. My heart ignites and thumps into overdrive. Blood throbs like a kick drum across my temples. Muzak whines around me like killer mosquitoes. I cut a sharp right and begin working my way up the north corridor.

Three steps further and I've moved into another state of existence completely.

I've spent countless hours wandering these waxy floors over the past few years, but right this second the Onion River Mall is a whole new world. I'm not just some mall rat killing time. I'm working—and I've got the cash to prove it. Ten bucks. A pale green portrait of President Alexander Hamilton. It's not much money for what I'm about to do, but, then, it's better than nothing, which is what I had when I walked in here about an hour ago.

I pushed the Chair for an Andrew Jackson—twenty beans—but he wouldn't meet my price. He's a slick negotiator, the Chair. That's why he's the best salesman in the whole mall. That's also why the other salespeople call him the Chair: He can get somebody from "Just

1

looking, thanks" to sitting down in a chair to try on shoes like no one this mall's ever seen before.

Slipping into customer traffic, I scan for maneuvering room. I don't need anyone getting in my way. I've got a job to do. This is my territory. This is *my* mall.

As I pass His New Look and breeze through an invisible cloud of cheap-leather vapors wafting from the store racks, I sense movement across the corridor, bodies pulling away from one another, creating gaps. I weave through the light crowd—the dregs of a so-so back-to-school shopping season. Space opens up as I pass SoundWaves, giving me a good twenty yards of unobstructed cruising past Jade Imports Ltd. and Hattie's Attic. A quick cut back into a smaller gap down the center of the corridor, and I spot the Ginger bulldozing toward the northwest exit.

A *Ginger* is what the Chair calls lady customers who are obsessed with the way their feet look in a pair of shoes. I don't really know what the term *Ginger* means, since the Chair has his own special language for describing retail work, but I know he'd like payback for the torture this Ginger just administered to him. That's where I come in— me and Alexander Hamilton.

Lucky for us, the Ginger's parked out back.

The mental picture of the dark northwest parking lot slams a gate in my mind, obliterating the last squeak of rubber on tile, the last whiny kid in new clothes wrenching a parent's arm, the last mosquito whine of Muzak. For me, the mall falls silent. Faces drift by like ghoulish balloons, and the fifty yards separating me from the Ginger, who heaves her girth against the exit door like a bronco ramming against its pen, becomes a simple series of inter-locking spaces, valves opening and closing in a pattern I can almost predict one step in advance. I spot an angular passage funneling into Big Buy, where I can make up time down the anchor store's long, straight aisles. I plunge into it.

After passing through Big Buy and exiting the mall, I've gained enough lead time on the Ginger to rest a few seconds and fill my lungs with the crisp evening air. The breeze presses my sweatshirt against my body. The sky is a swirling charcoal canopy, as if the clouds over Shunpike Falls are gathering to watch the hit go down, like kids crowding around a fight.

The northwest exit disgorges my prey.

I slip between rows of cars and zigzag toward her.

Only one row of cars separates us when the Ginger finally stops at a vehicle: a big, white, square sedan—a milk carton with wheels, basically. Drawing a few steps nearer, I hear her humming a tune. I crouch down and creep around the back of a minivan parked two cars over. Peeking through the minivan's windows, I watch her standing at her door, listen to her humming and fumbling for her keys. And I wait. At the sound of her door hinges creaking, I move in.

She turns, startled.

I tense up, thinking she might scream.

The moment passes with a soft, low whoop of wind.

"What do you want?" the Ginger grumbles, looking me up and down before settling her stink-eye on the torn pocket of my jeans, then on my Chuck Taylors, which aren't exactly new either. "I can't help you," she says with

3

a snort and begins turning back to her car. "Go away—"

"*Caveat emptor,*" I announce, just as the Chair told me to. Whatever the words mean, they make the Ginger's caterpillar eyebrows nearly jump into her black squirrel's nest of hair.

"What did you say—"

"*Caveat emptor,*" I repeat and advance a step.

Pressing a hand to her breast, she shrinks into her half-open door.

"*Caveat . . .*"—as I speak, traffic, people, time, and the wind all seem to freeze in place— "*. . . emptooor.*" The voice that seethes at her—low, even, not the donkey bray I'm used to hearing honk from my mouth—sounds only slightly familiar. "*Caveat emptor.*" The back of my neck tingles. My head feels light. "*Caveat emptor.*"

As the Ginger presses herself harder into her car door, her face a distorted mess of cosmetic seams and fear, I catch sight of my shadow on the pavement: a menacing black form, a bitter scarecrow come to life—coiled and ready to pounce. "*Caveat emptor!*" I raise my hand as if to take an oath, and the woman flinches.

I take a half step closer and raise my other hand. "*Caveat . . .*" My voice grows louder, more gravelly. "*. . . emptor!*"

As the Ginger draws another sharp breath, I spread my arms out at my sides and jab my hands in the air like a wizard summoning lightning bolts. My baggy sleeves make shadow wings on the pavement—vampire bat wings.

With a choking whimper, the Ginger scrambles into her car, slams the door, and trips the electric door locks. She

4

gawks at me through her window like some mutant creature in a jar.

Hearing her muffled shriek through the glass snaps me out of my daze. I dart for the bushes separating the mall parking lot from the bank next door. Someone beeps a horn, but I don't stop.

Branches rake my arms raw as I flee, scrambling through the bushes, unable to slow down. *Go*, is all I can think, my heart pounding in my chest like a sledgehammer against the side of a submarine.

Go.

As if I've become the hunted.

2

Mom's peeling vegetables at the kitchen sink when I walk in the front door. She doesn't say anything, though. She must be mad at me. I'm a little late. It's seven o'clock. We try to eat at six.

"Hi, Mom," I say.

She turns around and wipes loose hair out of her face. Her hair's pinned up with takeout chopsticks, and in the butter-yellow light of the kitchen I can see silver strands weaving through the black. Some nights I think I can tell she's getting older. "Hey, Mitch," she says, glancing at my jeans. "You're pushing it, timewise."

"Sorry."

"And those pants are getting a little ratty, don't you think? Since when is it okay to go to school looking like that?"

I shrug. "We don't have a dress code. At least not one that I know about—"

"Well, I don't want you wearing those jeans, understand?"

"But a lot of other kids—"

"You are *not* a lot of other kids." She bangs the vegetable peeler on the counter, just missing the glass of wine

6

sitting next to the sink. The noise seems to frighten her more than it does me.

Mom doesn't get mad very often, or at least she doesn't usually show it, but lately she's seemed on edge. I'm not sure why.

"You're my kid," she says in a slightly ragged voice. "Understand?"

It's clearly not a good night for debating with Mom, not that it ever is. She's pretty amped about something. And I doubt it's something as simple as my torn jeans or being late for dinner. I just pray she doesn't know about the Ginger—not impossible in a town the size of Shunpike Falls, where bad news gets around faster than a fire truck. But, then, that's probably being paranoid. "Yes," I say. "I understand."

"I don't like you walking around looking like you just don't care," Mom goes on. "Because if you don't care, that makes it look like I don't care. Know what I mean?"

"Yes."

"Good. Now go wash up." She turns back to the sink. "We're eating in ten."

≈

I wash my hands and splash cold water on my face, then look in the mirror for a few moments. I look guilty. I try a couple more splashes, but the look doesn't go away. It's pretty subtle, but I can see it. Did Mom see it?

I sit on the edge of the bathtub and try to get the Ginger's horrified face out of my mind. *Caveat emptor.* What does it mean? Would Mom know? Should I ask her?

Have I lost my mind?

Had I lost it even before I went to see the Chair?

7

The decision to stop by ShUSA seemed rational enough at the time. But, then, I've said that about a lot of things in my fifteen years of life that turned out not to be so rational after all. Here was my thought process, if you can even call it that:

I'm flat broke—*was* flat broke, I should say. I thought the Chair might have a solution to my problem. He's helped me out in the past, teaching me the three most important words in a kid's employment vocabulary:

under

the

table

Money paid to someone *under* the table doesn't get reported to the government. It's about the only way to hire a kid younger than sixteen. It's illegal, of course. Even though the under-the-table arrangement the Chair and I had going at ShUSA fell apart about a month after it started, I was banking on him having some other ideas up his suit sleeve. He's a quick thinker—kind of harsh sometimes, but smart when it comes to business.

Clearly, though, he was facing his own dilemma when I strolled in: the Ginger.

For a couple of seconds, I thought ShUSA was completely empty—no salespeople, no customers, no Chair. Then I found him down on the floor in Ladies Formals, directly beneath the "Steppin' Out" banner, straightening a woman's nylons. I could tell, from the pink shade in his ears and cheeks as he scrambled around his customer's feet, that she'd been keeping him busy for a while. From where I stood, over by the ShU-ShU the Choo-Choo display, the Chair reminded me of King Kong in that old

8

movie I caught on late-night TV: trapped there in a little city of canary yellow shoeboxes. The thirty or so ladies' shoes scattered around could've been cars the big ape had already crushed.

For the time being, though, the Chair seemed calm, which wasn't that surprising. While he'd earned his nickname for being what the mall salespeople call "a closer"— as in *deal* closer—he's no less legendary for keeping his salesman's cool, never letting customers rattle his nerves. Still, I wondered if this would be the Ginger that broke him. I mean, he'd shown her a *lot* of shoes. Boxes also filled the seat to the Ginger's left. A fur coat looking like stitched-together roadkill lay in a beaver-sized clump in the seat to her right.

"Now, keep in mind," I heard the Chair say as he sliced off a smile, "that when these shoes stretch, which they will do fairly quickly, your foot will *sliiide* forward slightly." With one hand he flicked something from the leg of his blue suit, then ran his fingers through his corporate-looking brown hair. His other hand reached for a box under the Ginger's seat.

I caught a glimpse of the black shoe as he pulled back the sheets of its tissue-paper nest: a narrow style with a tall heel and tiny strap. Just looking at it made my feet ache.

The Ginger nodded in a way that gave no clue as to whether she liked the shoe, hated the shoe, or expected the Chair to kiss her feet.

The Chair caught my eye, his expression oozing two seconds' worth of pure, distilled disgust before he took the Ginger's hand and helped her up.

9

I remember she did a wobbly turn to her left and walked toward the front of the store, teetering like someone trying to stand up in a rowboat.

"Now," the Chair practically sang to her as she made her way toward the mall corridor, "how do those feel to us?"

"*Uhnnn,*" the Ginger whined as she reached the edge of the carpet.

"They look very nice," the Chair added.

Staring at her feet, the Ginger mumbled something that sounded, from where I stood, like "mere."

The Chair didn't respond.

"Bring the *mirror,*" she snapped, glaring down the row of chairs, holding her arms out at her sides for balance.

"Why, certainly." The Chair gestured to the wall across from the mess of boxes. "We have a mirror right over here."

"No," the woman said with that little snort. "Up *here.*"

"Excuse me—"

"The mirror. Bring it . . . *here.*"

The Chair shot me a lightning-quick, flamethrower glance. "Why, of course," he said with a chuckle, as if he was being such a bonehead to expect the Ginger to walk *alll* the way back to her seat to look at the shoes in a mirror.

Taking his time, acting completely mellow about the whole deal, the Chair walked over to the wall, bent down, picked up the mirror, and carried it to the front of the store. Reaching the Ginger, he leaned the mirror against a chair leg next to her feet. "Now," he said in a soothing, radio deejay voice, "how do those suit us?"

10

Arms still out at her sides, the Ginger turned to the left, then to the right, examining the shoes in the mirror. After about a dozen of these pirouettes, she took a few unsteady steps back toward her seat. Suddenly she stopped and fixed the Chair with a "Don't just stand there" scowl.

"Elegant," he said with a grin and a wink.

The Ginger looked at the mirror, shifted her attention back to her feet, then shot the Chair that stink-eye again.

He smiled at her even harder, then lunged forward suddenly, bending one knee like a swordfighter making a thrust. "Hold on there, miss," he said with another dorky laugh as he picked the mirror up off the floor. "You're getting *waaay* ahead of me."

Before he could set the mirror back down by the Ginger's feet, she was already walking away.

That's when things got bizarre.

The Chair crouched down and, like a crab, began walking alongside his customer, holding the mirror next to her feet as she went.

A tingle crawled down the back of my neck as I watched the Chair crab-walk along, the keys in his pocket jingling with each foot scuff on the carpet, a wheeze sneaking out of his perma-smile every other step.

Glancing into the mall, I spotted a couple of Fashion Focus salespeople standing at the front edge of their store, directly across from ShUSA, watching the Chair and his customer—a Ginger and her pet crab—working their way slowly, painfully, back to her pile of roadkill.

As the Ginger finally reentered her little harbor of shoeboxes and began turning her cargo ship of a body around to sit, the Chair shot me another glance, his face showing no trace of the footwear professional's "How can I help you?" confidence but, instead, the frantic look of a wild animal on a short leash.

Before the Ginger sat down, she stood in front of her seat while the Chair returned the mirror to its original place against the wall. Rising, he stood aside so that the woman could admire her feet's reflection. Crossing his arms and holding his chin in one hand, he studied the shoes. "Yes," he said with a nod. "I wasn't sure at first, but I am really beginning to *enjoy* those on you. And if you don't mind my saying so . . ."

I felt that strange neck tingle again.

". . . you have *lovely* feet."

The Ginger said nothing, didn't acknowledge the Chair's comment, but finally sat down. She lifted her left leg in the air.

The Chair dropped to one knee and pried the little black shoes off her. "Now, how did those feel to you?" he asked, straightening the toes of her nylons again. He set the shoes on top of their box, as if on a museum pedestal. "Because they sure looked *terrific.*"

"Tight," the woman replied.

"Well, perhaps we could try a nine—"

"Eight."

"Well, yes, this is an eight—"

"I'm an eight."

"Yes, of course, but remember that this particular shoe *is* cut a little narrower. Perhaps an eight and a half—"

"I'm not an eight and a half."

"No, clearly you're not. But keep in mind that it's the

end of the day, and your feet are likely a little . . . bloated."

Bloated.

The word hung in the air like ammonia vapors in a school bathroom. Right there, right then, it was exactly the wrong word for the situation. Almost any other word—*expanded* or even *swollen*—wouldn't have flooded the mind with the images that *bloated* did:

Bullfrogs croaking in the mud.

A kid who's overdone it at a pizza party.

Farm animals fattened up for slaughter.

The Chair's face, which had been glowing a light pink, turned as red as a stoplight. "I mean *swollen,*" he added, his voice cracking. "It's normal for feet to . . . *swell* slightly over the course of a day."

The Ginger glared at him.

"And, well, as I said, those particular shoes *are* cut a bit *narrower* than most. Are you sure you won't try—"

"No." The Ginger raised her leg again and placed it squarely on the Chair's knee. "I think I've tried my patience to its very end just by coming in here."

The Chair looked at her croquet-mallet foot as if expecting it to kick him in the teeth. He pulled from beneath her chair some worn, ankle-length, Peter Pan–type boots. With a few quick moves, he crammed her feet back into the boots and zipped one, then the other.

The Ginger rose to her feet, gathered up the roadkill coat, and, without a word, shoved it into the Chair's arms, turning her back to him. He helped her on with the coat, and she stampeded into the mall without so much as

13

a glance back—much less a "thank you."

And that's where I stepped in—sort of.

Except for the strains of Muzak, pierced by the occasional squeak of kids' shoes sprinting up and down the mall corridor, an uncomfortable silence hung over ShUSA. The Chair just stood in the middle of his little city of boxes, looking like he'd just been shot with a tranquilizer dart.

I walked over to him. "Whoa," I said. "You all right?"

He started to say something but couldn't seem to get the words out as he surveyed the boxes piled around him. He turned toward the Ginger's seat, the cushion of which was still flattened. "Well, that was rather unpleasant," he finally said in a rough whisper, almost as if talking to himself. "Now, there's a woman who left her manners at home. If only I could somehow help her . . . find them."

His creepy tone of voice made the back of my neck tingle again. Deep down in my ribs, I knew something bad was about to happen. "Take it easy, Chair," I said. "This is your job. You're a professional—"

"I'd like to tell her . . ."

"Tell her what? The customer's always right, remember?"

"Tell her that she's a . . ."

"You can't."

"Someone's got to."

"Impossible. You'll lose your job."

He locked on his reflection in the floor mirror. "She stepped over the line," he whispered in that rough voice again, shaking his head.

I noticed another customer walking into the store—a

14

tall, stern-looking man wearing a brown windbreaker, reading spectacles, and an unfriendly, "Let's talk price" face. The Chair, oblivious to the man's presence, let out a faint but definitely maniacal laugh and winked at himself in the mirror. "Hey, there," he said to his reflection. "Remember me?"

The disturbing cheerfulness in his voice started my blood really pumping. It dawned on me that the Chair wasn't talking to me or himself anymore. He was talking to the Ginger. And it wasn't nice.

Hearing the words spew from his mouth, I was actually afraid to tell him about Let's Talk Price—afraid for the customer's safety. The Chair swore into the mirror—and pretty loudly— which drew the customer's attention from across the store. I started focusing my mental energies on pushing the guy away, like a TV movie I saw about evil kids who could cause mass destruction just by thinking really hard about it. I let my mind race with things I could say to a customer on the front end of a retail transaction to stamp out any ideas of using a salesman for a stress dumpster, which is basically what Onion River Mall customers do.

The Chair swore again, and Let's Talk Price started making impatient sounds—obnoxious tongue clicks— from where he stood underneath the "ShUSport" banner. I could tell, just by the way he was standing—arms crossed, eyes fixed on the Chair over the tops of his specs—that he expected the Chair to race right over and help him. When the Chair kept on muttering to himself, the man let out an audible huff, shook his head, and turned around.

I sighed with relief. I thought I was going to have to insult the man—enough, at least, to get rid of him—just to save him from something worse.

That's when it hit me, like a soccer ball right in the face.

"Chair," I said, watching Let's Talk Price reach for a particularly cheesy style of ShUSA running shoe. "I have an idea."

". . . and I hope you'll think of me every time you pick up those crutches to come down to the mall," he hissed into the mirror.

"You don't really want to hurt that lady, do you?" I said, leaning so that my reflection was in the mirror too, a small mop of black hair hovering over his shoulder.

"Sure I do, Mitch. Very much."

"But do you have to?"

He cocked an eyebrow—a great improvement over the crazed look he'd been exchanging with himself in the mirror.

"What I mean is that you want revenge, right?"

"I will *have* revenge," he seethed.

"Yeah, but what's that expression? 'An eye for an eye, a tooth for a tooth.'"

The Chair's reflection nodded at me. "I'm familiar with that concept, yes. How does it apply here?"

"I have a proposal. Even though you can be pretty uptight sometimes, I still owe you for letting me work in the stockroom, at least until . . . well, you know." I glanced toward the darkened archway at the back of the store, next to the "ShUCare Corner" display, remembering the brief period when the Chair was paying me under the table to check in inventory shipments after school. The arrangement lasted about a month before that bitchy ShUSA regional manager—Gladys something, with the pointy chin—made her surprise visit just as I was unloading a truckload of Spring Casuals. If the Chair hadn't been a killer salesman, he later told me, our deal might've cost him his job. In the end, it only cost me *my* job.

The Chair's reflection cocked another eyebrow. "Go on."

"So, here's what I'm going to do. I'm going to run an errand for you. For a small fee, of course."

The Chair's smile twitched in the mirror. "You want to make some sort of deal, Mitch?"

"Sort of. But this isn't the kind of deal you walk away from with something . . . tangible."

"Then what's in it for me?"

"Well, how about peace of mind? How about . . . revenge?"

He turned to face me directly, and my heart jumped a couple of times, like a frog under a garbage bag. "Deal, kid."

I looked into the mall corridor. "Think about that Ginger. She's probably not even to the parking lot yet."

"What are you saying, Mitch?"

"Whatever you want me to say."

The Chair cracked the world's slightest smile, but I saw it. I know the guy's moods, his techniques, his way of showing you one face while hiding another. "You mean . . ."

"It's insult or be insulted," I said.

"Clever. Did you make that up?"

"No, I believe it was President . . ." I studied the Chair's expression, trying to gauge how angry he was at the Ginger, at the mall, at the world, at whatever. "I believe it was President . . . Andrew Jackson."

The Chair whistled. "Did you say Abraham Lincoln?"

"Jackson. Andrew Jackson."

The Chair adjusted his tie. "Are you sure you didn't say . . ." He gave the store a quick scan, as if making sure we weren't being watched. His eyes narrowed when he caught sight of Let's Talk Price. ". . . Alexander Hamilton?" The rough whisper was back.

I took a deep breath and tried to hold my ground, but after a few seconds I caved in. "Okay. It was Alexander Hamilton."

The Chair took a ladies' dress shoe off the rack in front of him—an ecru-colored item with a closed toe and sensible heel—then plunged his other hand into his pocket.

A second later, I caught sight of a ten-dollar bill flashing in the store's bright light, like a bird scared out of a shrub.

"You know, Alexander Hamilton believed in a strong central bank," the Chair said. "Evidently, so do you. Listen up." He stepped closer and proclaimed, as if making a toast, "*Caveat emptor.*" He poked me once in the chest with the ladies' shoe, then tossed it in the air.

I caught it and glanced inside. Alexander Hamilton peered up at me, as if waiting for a declaration to be dropped in there for him to sign.

"*Caveat emptor,*" the Chair repeated, giving me a very serious look.

I was just about to ask him what the words mean, but he started walking over to Let's Talk Price. "Good evening, sir," he said, straightening each suit sleeve with a firm tug. The upbeat, radio-deejay punch had returned to the Chair's voice. He practically bounced on his black shoes. "Looking for something in particular?"

You'd have thought it was his first customer of the day.

~

"Just one more minute, hon," Mom says when I walk back into the kitchen, so I set the table and light a couple of candles, which sometimes helps her relax after a hard day at Quadrangle, the printing plant in Quarry where she works, two towns down the Onion River. Just as I'm blowing out the match, she comes out of the kitchen, a plate of pasta in one hand, a bowl of salad in the other— and a concerned look on her face that could ruin my appetite if she doesn't cheer up.

I sit down, noticing how the candlelight accentuates the lines creasing her forehead and the corners of her mouth, making her look ten years older than she did this morning. More and more often, she comes home from Quadrangle missing large pieces of the woman who pulled out of the driveway in that noisy, rusty Volkswagen that morning.

"Smells good," I say as Mom sits down and pours herself some more wine.

"I'm glad you think so." She hands me the salad tongs. "I'm glad someone thinks I know what I'm doing." A second later, she sighs and rests her head on one hand. "I'm sorry, Mitch. You don't need to hear that."

"It's okay," I say, sorry she's bummed about something but relieved that what's bugging her is probably in *her* world, not mine. "Vent if you want to."

19

She smiles faintly, her head still resting on her hand. "I'll spare you the gory details. We're just really short-staffed in my department, and that's creating a lot more work for people, especially for me."

"Are they hiring?"

"Yes. But it's tough to find people right now."

"It's the economy," I say. "People won't work for that kind of money."

Mom winces and sits upright. "*That* kind of money happens to keep us fed and clothed—"

"Sorry. I didn't mean—"

"In spite of the way you insist on dressing—"

"Honest. I didn't mean it like that."

Mom frowns and sips her wine.

A jet approaches in the distance, and we both withdraw into our own private realms, like turtles hiding in our shells. When the roar is directly overhead, I look at Mom out of the corner of my eye, afraid that the rumbling along our windows, roof, and walls might loosen the dark cracks the candle has scrawled across her face, causing her to crumble into pieces. She stares blankly into the candlelight and chews—on autopilot.

"So," she says when the jet engines have faded to distant static, "how's the team stack up this season?"

I look at her, unsure how to answer.

She sips her wine and catches me staring. "*Hmm?*"

"Team?" I say.

"What's that?"

"You just asked me how the team stacks up?"

"I did?" Mom gazes into the living room, as if for some

reminder of why she said what she said. "Huh." She chuckles and turns back to her food. "I'm not sure what I was thinking."

I haven't been on any team since junior high school, two years ago, when I played soccer. It's true, I *tried out* for the Shunpike High team last season, my freshman year, but I got cut. A varsity letter I can live without, but what's the deal with Mom? She seems really spaced out tonight. And I don't think it's the wine. She rarely has more than a couple of glasses.

"What a crazy world," she says, looking down as if talking to the reflection in her plate.

"No doubt."

"I mean, there's some crazy stuff going on these days. Some of it really stupid, stupid stuff." A frightened look flashes in her eyes. "And I'd hate to see you get caught up in any of it."

"I'm not going to get caught up—"

"*Listen* to your mother," she snaps.

The sudden edge in her voice makes me swallow milk down the wrong tube, but I cover my mouth with my napkin just before spewing it all over the table.

"Sorry, honey," she says more softly. "You okay?"

I nod as I cough.

And that seems to be the end of it, a short but confusing conversation. As we finish eating, I try to piece it together—all the vague talk about some . . ."*stuff*" . . . going on. Does she or doesn't she know about the Ginger? I'm guessing . . . no. Is she okay, though? She's acting really weird. Should I be worried?

21

Another jet approaches, and we fall silent again. Every few seconds I sneak a glance at Mom. She still seems worried about something. As soon as the jet noise has faded, I have to ask her: "Everything okay, Mom?"

"Oh, yeah, I'll be fine." She reaches over to pat the back of my hand. "Thanks. I was just thinking about something I heard today. An old man up on Valley Road. Someone beat him up. Did you hear about this?"

"No."

Mom gazes into the living room again. "I wasn't sure if you'd heard or not. He was sixty-five, seventy, I guess. Just walking along, minding his own business."

"Is he all right?"

"Oh, they worked him over pretty good. Took his wallet, his watch. But I guess he'll live."

"He'll *live?* My god—"

"Yeah, he's in critical condition. 'Critical but stable,' they said on the news."

"Do they know who did it?"

She looks at me for a second, then down at her plate again. "Someone mentioned Jimmy Biggins."

"They always mention Jimmy," I grumble, the words leaping out of my mouth before I can soften them up.

Mom closes her eyes as if preparing to break some very bad news, as if there's anything about Jimmy Biggins she could tell me that I don't already know. "Well, he *has* been in some trouble, Mitch."

"Jimmy had nothing to do with it." I take a long drink of milk to keep from saying something I'll regret. "This guy, this old man," I add, working to stay calm, "did he give any description?"

Mom shakes her head. "He was completely blindsided. Anyway, the police didn't catch him, them, whoever it was." She takes a sip of wine. "I'm telling you, things have gotten crazy around here."

We're silent awhile longer. As we finish dinner, I have to admit to myself that Mom is dead-on right—in one way, anyway. Things have gotten worse in Shunpike Falls in the last few years. Some gangs have started up, including some skinheads called Next of Skin, which I don't remember there being when I was still in middle school. Since Shunpike Falls is in the middle of nowhere and almost nothing serious ever happens here, we don't have metal detectors at school . . . yet. But plenty of kids carry knives and guns. A couple of guys had their lockers raided last year, but no one's actually used a weapon in school . . . yet. I'm sure Mom has read all about it in the *Onion River Beacon,* our town's weekly newspaper, which, to be honest, is a lot less annoying than having her pump me for information about what's happening around town.

My history teacher, Mr. LaGasse—"Mr. Bad Gas," as he's known—calls the *Beacon* editor, Mrs. Pegg, a "yellow journalist" and a "gossip monger." I don't read the paper often enough to have an opinion about it, but if the *Beacon* gives my parents something to do instead of prying into my personal matters, then I'm all for it.

When we're both finished eating, Mom takes our plates into the kitchen. As I put the pasta bowl and our glasses into the empty salad bowl, images pour into my mind: the Ginger's craggy-makeup face grimacing from inside her car; an old man lying in a hospital bed with tubes running out of his nose; Alexander Hamilton's stony expression

23

against a greenish white background. I stare into the candlelight, trying to make the images disappear.

I know that one of those images—old Alexander Hamilton—will disappear, for real, soon enough. Then what?

"You okay, Mitch?" Mom says from the doorway to the kitchen.

"Yeah." I fake a yawn. "I'm just beat. I think I'll get started on my homework."

"Okay, but . . . It's just . . ."

"Just what?" I walk past her and into the kitchen.

"Your father said he was going to stop by."

I don't respond right away as I slip the glasses and bowls into the sudsy water pooled on one side of the sink. "Since when does he need an appointment?"

"That tone of voice concerns me."

"Tonight?"

"That's what he said."

"Any idea what time?"

Mom looks at her watch. "Well, actually, he should be here by now."

"That's my dad." Passing Mom again on my way back to the table, I mumble, "Whatever." It just slips out.

"Now, Mitch, be fair."

Shaking my head, I catch my distorted reflection in one of the brass candleholders. "Fair. Speaking of fair—"

"Don't start, please—"

"If he comes over, the question is will my fair-minded father possibly—"

"I asked you not to—"

"Will he possibly have anything for you? You, who

24

have been *more than* fair, I'd say. I mean, he isn't contributing anything to this household, is he?"

Mom puts her hands over her nose and mouth, as if making a wish, counting to ten, praying. "Let's not get into that. Anyway, he doesn't live here."

"How can we not 'get into that'? And by the way, I *do* live here, and *he* happens to be *my* father, and *we* could use a little financial help—"

"He hasn't got any money—you know that. And the financial arrangements he and I have made don't need to be any of your business either."

Business. The word is like a punch in the stomach. "Business," I mutter without really thinking about what I'm saying, the ten-dollar bill in my pocket seeming to gouge me like a pencil. "What are we, the damn Chamber of Commerce?"

"You will *not* talk that way in this house!" Mom shouts, then retreats into the kitchen.

Another jet approaches, the thunderous engines like boulders being dropped on the roof. The dim candlelight makes the room feel like a cave, a cave getting smaller with each rumble overhead.

I turn to step outside for some air and nearly run into my father letting himself in.

"Hey, buddy," he says above the roar.

I fake a smile. "Hey, Dad." As I sit back down and we both wait for the noise to die out, my nostrils catch a whiff of aftershave. I give Dad a quick inspection: Noticeably thinner than when I saw him a few weeks ago, he swims in his worn, brown work pants and a white shirt streaked with coffee and mustard stains. He's wearing those cheap ShUSA running shoes and gray socks—not a real strong fashion statement. Flecks of paint dot the backs of his hands and the bald spot flanked by wild tufts of gray-brown hair.

As my eyes linger on his scraggly beard and the dark circles under his eyes, he turns away. "Sounds like I barged in right in the middle of something," he says.

"Oh, it was nothing. I was being a brat. Sorry, Mom."

Mom's watching us from the sink, as if expecting a made-for-TV-movie reunion: "Thanks, Mitch," she says. "I'm sorry too."

"Well, all's well that ends well," Dad says with a clap. "That's what's important."

Mom steps into the kitchen doorway. "Can I get you anything, Reg?"

Dad looks at her. "No, thanks, Sally. I'm all set." He turns back to me but lowers his eyes. "I just came by to . . . well . . . I need to talk to the Big M here about something—"

"About what?" I say so quickly that Dad's eyes widen. My heart revs up like a motorcycle. If anyone in town could find out about the Ginger, my father would be that person. Among the many things he is here in Shunpike Falls—a loser, a joke, pathetic—he's also as nosy as a police dog.

"Well . . ." Dad pulls a chair out from the dining room table and sits down. "I suppose you've heard by now. The man up on Valley Road."

I quietly let out the deep breath I've been holding in. "He didn't do it," I say. "Jimmy Biggins didn't do it."

Dad gives me a wary look. "How do you know that,

Mitch? The kid's been in all kinds of trouble—"

"Because I know him, that's how."

"Jimmy's a friend of Mitch's," Mom says.

Dad turns to her, then back to me. "Well," he declares, pointing at me, "you should be more careful who you make friends with."

Before I realize what I'm doing, I point right back at him. "You're one to talk. Some friends your old business partners turned out to be." I rocket out of my seat and into the kitchen.

No one speaks for a few moments, which is fine with me. My heart's about to knock something over through my rib cage.

"So, I take it," Dad continues in a more cautious tone, "you don't know anything about this Valley Road incident?"

"No," I say, trying not to sound too snotty, "just what Mom told me about ten minutes ago."

Dad doesn't respond for a while. Out of the corner of my eye, I see him peeling paint off his fingertips. Mom and I look at each other again, but she looks away, as if ashamed. Of me? Of herself? Of Dad? I can't really tell.

"Sorry, Mitch," Dad finally says. "I should butt out."

"You don't have to butt out, Dad. Just—"

"It's just . . . I get a little . . . well, I'm just trying to make sure you're okay. You know, this town . . ." He turns to my mother as she passes by, a dish rag in her hand. "Can you believe this place, Sal? Can you?"

"It's sad." Mom sighs, tossing the rag onto the dining room table and wiping it down. "It's not the place we grew up in, that's for sure. Nobody cares anymore."

27

"We don't *know* each other anymore," Dad says, his mouth and eyes sagging. "That's the problem. Look at the way this town has developed. Where do we ever just bump into each other? Huh? When do we slow down long enough to just *be* with each other?"

Mom sighs again and looks at Dad with an almost identical sad light in her eyes. On her way past him and back into the kitchen, she gives his shoulder a squeeze. It's the first time I've seen her touch him in . . . I don't remember the last time. I know that Mom and Dad have some serious differences to work out, but a little gesture like that makes me realize that we're still more or less a family.

"And that mall isn't helping," Dad says with more edge in his voice.

Mom turns quickly at the sink and faces him. "Reg, maybe not tonight, okay? Let's not talk about the mall."

The mall. My heart nearly jumps out of my mouth and onto the table. *What about the mall?*

Fortunately, Dad takes Mom's suggestion and just looks at the floor as if he's been scolded. "The point is, Mitch," he says a few seconds later, "your Mom and I just want you to be safe, to be happy."

"I know," I say. "And I'm doing fine. How are you doing?"

Dad looks at me but hesitates to respond. He runs his paint-flecked hands through his paint-flecked hair and stares at the ceiling as another jet approaches. When the roar has passed overhead and subsided, he claps his hands around his thighs and gives me that ever-hopeful wink he

28

throws out from time to time. "What do you say we talk about something a little more cheerful?" he says. "Enough of that Valley Road business."

Business. The Ginger's twisted face pops into my thoughts again like a piece of burnt toast.

"Tell me," Dad chirps with so much false cheer that I want to throw myself through the kitchen window and into the backyard, "how's school going?"

3

Page is writing something, her tray pushed aside, when I find her in the cafeteria. Her black eyebrows make two arrows aimed at her notebook. She wears her black braid tucked under the collar of her brown suede jacket—the one her mother gave her, with the fringes on the sleeves. Page once told me that her mother wore that same jacket in her college days, when supposedly she was really into protesting. Ms. Anderson called it her "activist armor." So when Mr. Anderson had an affair and split town last year, Page's mom—Wanda, she lets us call her now—handed the jacket down to Page, I guess as a reminder never to get too comfortable with the way things are.

No one who knows Page would ever say she's too comfortable with the way things are. I've known her since we were nine, when she played on my Peanut League baseball team. She was the only girl in the league, of course, because she refused to play softball. She was a pretty good infielder, and she got her share of hits, if I remember correctly.

"What's up?" I say, tossing my backpack into one of the empty chairs at her table.

"Hey." She frowns and cocks her head, her lips moving silently as she reads.

"You know, they call it *home*work for a reason," I say, imitating what our English teacher, Mr. Framm, always says when he catches someone scribbling out an assignment in class that should've been completed beforehand.

"You're quite a comedian," Page says flatly, her eyes still fixed on the notebook. Finally, after another couple seconds of rereading, she sets her pen down, flexes her writing hand, and looks at me. "What's up?"

"Have you seen Jimmy?"

Page doesn't say anything, just narrows her eyes.

I figure she's heard the Valley Road rumors. "He didn't do it," I say.

"Can you confirm that?"

"Since when do I have to confirm it? Isn't someone innocent until proven guilty?"

Page stares at me for a couple more seconds, then looks across the cafeteria, toward the window facing the athletics equipment shed. "I don't like that kid."

"No one likes him," I say.

Page turns back to me. "You like him."

"We went to kindergarten together." As I say this, I realize that it doesn't fully explain why Jimmy and I are still friends. To be honest, I see less and less of him these days, and just hanging out with him is likely to get a person in some kind of trouble. "What are you writing?" I say, changing the subject.

"A letter." Page tears the sheet of paper from her notebook and eyes it with concern, as if considering whether

31

she should rip it up or frame it. "It's to Mr. Beaner."

"The *River's Edge* advisor."

"Yes. I feel that a school newspaper should be interested in more than sports, particularly *boys'* sports."

"Now that you mention it, the football team's been the cover story since school started—"

"Oh, I know. Believe me, I know. Worst early-season record in the school's history. Meanwhile, the women's soccer team is undefeated." Page squints coldly at me, as if I'm the *River's Edge* editor—an idea that would make Mr. Framm bust a rib laughing.

"That's lame," I say, but without much conviction, since just as the words are forming in my brain I spot Tammy Bernard's toothpaste-commercial smile filling the glass of the cafeteria door. Even more startling, she seems to be waving at me. I look around to see if she could be waving at someone else. Her boyfriend, Mark Walters, the football team's starting linebacker, would be the most likely candidate, or at least someone from the junior or senior class. Certainly not me. But she stands there waving until I wave back. Then she moves on.

"Since when are you and Tammy Bernard such good friends?" Page says.

"Since about ten seconds ago. That was weird."

"Maybe she likes younger men. Shorter men. Men with squeaky voices—"

"Who's the comedian now?"

Page smirks and folds her letter into thirds.

A hand on my shoulder startles me. I turn around, expecting to see Jimmy standing there with some goofy look on his face, but instead it's Keith Sullivan—or, rather, Keith Sullivan's belt, since Keith is about seven feet tall. "Whazzup, Mitch Graham?" he says, extending one of his catcher's-mitt-size hands.

I shake his hand and gaze up into his cloud of curly red hair, resisting the temptation to correct him: *"Uh, it's Grant, not Graham."* The acne scattered across his chalky-white forehead looks like a swarm of gnats dancing in the glow of a bug light.

I give Page a quick look. She's staring up at Keith too, her mouth hanging open slightly. It's a natural reaction to being up close to such a rare physical specimen as Keith, not that I've been close to him that many times. In fact, I don't think we've ever even exchanged words. I'm sure of it. He's a senior, a cocaptain of the basketball team, and likely to end his athletic career at Shunpike Falls High School the all-time leading scorer. I not only did not make the varsity soccer team but was strongly discouraged from clogging up the junior varsity roster.

"You all right, kid," Keith says in that grammatically incorrect way that the basketball team says things, even though half the squad made the National Honor Society last season. He points a beer-bottle-size finger at me as he moves along. "You *alll* right."

I turn back to Page and zone out on her tray, trying to read in the fork-scratch graffiti some explanation for why not only Tammy Bernard but now Keith Sullivan would seek me out for a friendly hello. Page, probably just as puzzled by these developments as I am, doesn't say anything.

33

And they truly are puzzling developments. I mean, if our school were the sky, Keith and Tammy would be stars in some major constellation, like the Big Dipper, the Little Dipper, or that cluster of seven stars . . . I forget what they're called. Anyway, I wouldn't even be a star. I'd be a trace of space gas, probably in another galaxy, one far beyond the view of even the strongest telescope.

Yet there is one thing connecting us, it dawns on me as I notice two freshmen dudes in brand-new Kourt Kingz basketball shoes squeaking toward the dish room.

Last week, just for a joke, Jimmy and I each tried on a pair of Kingz at the mall. What made it funny was the way we impersonated each other's parents when we imagined asking them to buy us a pair of Kingz—the most expensive basketball shoes known to man. Jimmy thinks his dad paid less money for the family car, which sounds about right, considering the shape that car is in—not that my parents ride in style or anything.

Yes, that's definitely it, the thing that links Keith, Tammy, and me: the Onion River Mall.

Keith works at Off the Bench Sports.

Tammy works at Rings 'n' Things.

I took a coat of paint off a Ginger in the parking lot last night.

"Popular guy today," Page says, tucking the letter to Mr. Beaner inside her jacket as she gets up.

"Seems that way."

"What's your secret?"

I shrug my shoulders, since I really don't know what all this means—not exactly. I mean, nothing I can *confirm*.

"Well, I'm going to leave so your fan club will have some-where to sit," Page says, picking up her tray. "But if you're not too busy signing autographs later, let's hang out."

"Cool," I say, suddenly feeling a little dizzy—from hunger or confusion, maybe a mixture of both. "Meet me at the mall."

"Sure," Page says, "for something new and exciting."

4

I enter the mall through Big Buy and begin scanning for the Ginger. She seemed totally wigged by our confrontation last night, but I'm not going to assume I scared her off for good. She was pretty nasty to the Chair. She might be a fighter.

Not watching where I'm going, I'm almost run over by Stu, one of the RediGard security guys. His olive-colored uniform flashes across my view like the door of a passing army truck. I jump out of his way and get ready to run as he looks back over his beefy shoulder.

Stu keeps lumbering along, though, in his brick-size shoes. "Slow down" is all he says. As he scratches at his black buzzcut, I can hear Lance Hungerford, the mall security chief, barking orders through Stu's radio, as if driving him around by remote control. I listen for Lance to say my name, but, thankfully, he doesn't. Stu disappears into the flow of mall traffic, and I move along, just a bit more slowly.

Cruising past Dapper Daze and Candy Man, however, I do hear someone call my name—an unfamiliar female voice. I look around but don't see anyone. When I hear my name again, just as I'm passing Hattie's Attic, I nearly trip.

Leaning out from Hattie's is Maggie St. Germaine—known throughout the mall as "the Hattie's Hotty." She's beckoning me with one hand and adjusting an earring with the other. "Hi, Mitch," she says with a toss of her wavy, strawberry-blond hair. "Got a second?"

"Not right now," I answer, although that's not exactly true, and pick up the pace again.

There's definitely something weird going on. It's as if I've stepped into a parallel universe where the most insignificant people are the most popular. No offense to Maggie St. Germaine, but I'm not sure I like it. That tingle running down my neck makes me think there might be a catch.

Page and Marcus are easy to spot in the mall atrium, especially Marcus: He's one of only three African American kids in our school, and his family, the Walkers, are one of roughly that many black families in all of Shunpike Falls. He and Page are sitting on one of the benches beside the fountain under the atrium skylight. Marcus is wearing a brown tweed coat, which he's been doing since school started—patches on the elbows, the whole bit. With his glasses on, he could pass for a teacher—that is, as long as he's sitting down. He and I are still lagging behind in the height department.

As I near the bench, I notice that Marcus and Page are staring off into space, both of them looking angry. Marcus has his arms crossed. "Hey," I say as I reach them.

Page mutters a faint "Hey, Mitch" but mostly gives

me a look—a look that says something's wrong.

"What's up, Marcus?"

He sighs heavily, uncrosses his arms, rests his hands on the knees of his forest green corduroys. "Security," he says, turning to me with an expression that suggests I should know what he means.

"What about security?" I say. "It's not very good here at the mall. But, then, neither is business."

"Well, let me tell you, as a black man, I disagree with that opinion."

"What—"

"I happen to have firsthand knowledge of just how tight security can be here at the mall." He stares ahead again, recrosses his arms, and doesn't say anything else.

Page gestures with a nod down the south corridor. "Marcus thinks one of Lance's security guards, the short one with the mustache—"

"Armand."

"Right. Anyway, he's been following Marcus around, you know—"

"Because I'm black." Marcus finishes Page's thought.

I don't know what to say in this situation, so I don't say anything right away. "Well, that guy's an idiot anyway," I finally muster.

"*And* a racist," Marcus huffs.

I wait another couple of moments, hoping Marcus cools down. I'm no good with this kind of stuff, racial stuff. Not many people in Shunpike Falls are, since everyone here is pretty much the same shade of pasty white.

The more I think about it, though, the more I realize that I sometimes get followed around by security too. So does Jimmy. A lot of kids do, especially kids from the Airport neighborhood, since we tend to dress like we don't have any money to spend—mainly because we *don't* have any money to spend. Lance and his troops must think we're more likely to shoplift. I suppose that's generally true. Generally.

Page recommends that Marcus write a letter to the *Beacon* about being racially profiled here at the mall. She's all about the angry letters these days. Her voice fades into the background of my thoughts as I spot two Queensbury Prep couples making their way up the south corridor.

I don't actually know any kids who go to Queensbury Prep, which is on the Queensbury College campus, just across the Onion River from the mall and on top of a hill. But for some reason I still get a little annoyed when I see them here in the mall. Maybe it's the fact that Queensbury Prep kids *come down* to shop here that bugs me, as if their little hilltop campus puts them above us in other ways.

Something about these two couples lazing along, weaving through the traffic with an almost waltzing motion, draws me in. The dudes, wearing maroon and white Queensbury Crew jackets and beat-up baseball hats, walk in front of the girls. Every few seconds one of the guys punches the other in the shoulder, while their girlfriends laugh, squeaking like dolphins and swinging their shopping bags like baskets of Easter candy. As I track them, the other sights and sounds of the mall seem to die down, leaving only the dudes' goofy voices, interrupted by the slap of knuckles on wool, and the girls' birdlike laughter, interrupted by nothing in the world. There's something calming about the way the four of them drift to one side of the mall, then to the other, hovering near the occasional pushcart, circling once or twice. Life is good.

The taller of the girls takes a cell phone from her purse and holds it to her ear, her perfect cut of sandy blond hair resembling, from a distance, a bicycle helmet. Suddenly she turns in my direction. When our eyes meet, she frowns, cocking her head to one side. "*Creep.*" I imagine her snotty voice echoing through the corridor. I look away, feeling my ears heat up, feeling like I've just been reprimanded in a way I haven't been in a long time, not since the last time Jimmy and I got caught pool-hopping.

I turn back to Marcus and Page but notice, behind them, Andy Briggs standing near the edge of SoundWaves, the electronics store between Yarn Barn and Dapper Daze. He's waving a slip of paper that, even from this distance, I can tell is cash.

"Don't you think so, Mitch?" Page says. "Don't you think Marcus should write a letter? At least then the complaint would be recorded somewhere."

"Sounds good," I say as Andy ducks back inside the store.

"You weren't really listening, were you?" Page grumbles.

"No," I say, watching Andy approach a customer. "Not really."

"You don't care that one of your best friends is a victim of racial discrimination?" Marcus says, his voice creeping up into that high range that he sometimes uses to emphasize outrage. Fortunately, he isn't usually outraged at me.

"Sure, I care," I say, catching Andy giving me another

40

quick look, then a wave toward the store. "But right now I have a little business to take care of."

"Business?" Page says. "What kind of business?"

"Customer service." I scan the mall for RediGard olive uniforms. Clear. "Meet me at the Mound in a half-hour, and I'll tell you all about it."

～

Four customers are dispersed like compass points throughout SoundWaves, but Andy appears to be the only salesperson on the floor. I take up a position in the east, next to a showcase of headphones a couple of feet from where he's helping a fidgety woman in a scratchy-looking beige overcoat pick out a stereo.

The woman squints at the speakers, waiting for music to come out. When it finally does, it sounds like a home recording of a kid playing the *Star Wars* theme on the trombone.

I fight back a laugh, remembering how I was forced to learn that song in the trombone section of the Shunpike Falls Middle School band. I didn't think it was such a bad song, really, but by that point in my music career I was pretty sick of the tarnished old horn—the same one Dad had played in his junior high school band in, like, the late-eighteenth century. When he moved out of the house the summer before I started at Shunpike High, I tucked the trombone back into its moldy old case and put it down in the basement. Neither he nor Mom seemed to notice that I'd stopped lugging it in and out of the house. Or maybe they just had a number of other things to deal with. Like each other, for example.

"No, no, I don't think so," the woman says with a

rapid-fire shake of her narrow, vaguely dachshund-like head.

"Now, it's a bit difficult to do," Andy croons, dabbing at some sweat trickling down from his blond sideburns, "but let's try to sort out the quality of the *recording* from the quality of the *playback*—"

"That one." Dachshunda points to another stereo. "I'd like to hear it in that one."

"Absolutely." Andy catches my eye as he asks the woman, "And how long has your son been playing the trombone?"

"This is his second year in the Middle School band," she says, just as proud as can be.

I cringe, remembering the noise the trombone section of the Shunpike Falls Middle School band made in our second year together. And Dachshunda's kid is no prodigy.

Andy's obviously trying very hard to help the lady, but he has to turn away every thirty seconds or so to help the other customers demanding his attention from north, south, and west. During one frantic trip between Dachshunda and some beefy guy in a Red Sox jacket three sizes too small for him, Andy presses a ten-dollar bill into my hand. "Get her," he says, his ordinarily friendly voice as rough as sandpaper.

I watch him blow right by the lady. Naturally, Dachshunda gives him the stink-eye, huffs and puffs, hands on her hips—the works—then storms out of the store.

I give her a count of ten before following.

Why am I doing this? Don't get me wrong: If somebody offered me a job here at the Onion River Mall, I'd take it in a heartbeat. Sure, I'd rather not work in a girl's store, like Hattie's Attic or Fashion Focus, but I'd probably still do it if it was the only job I could get. Maybe I could do something with the inventory back in the stockroom, where no one would see me, like I did at ShUSA for a brief period. A job's a job, a chance to make a few bucks. That's a chance I could use right about now. Thing is, Dachshunda's the only offer I've had today.

She slows down near the atrium, takes a look down the south corridor—the bottom of the *L* that makes the Onion River Mall. I slow down too, pretending to check out sunglasses at a pushcart fifty feet or so away from her.

The salesperson working the cart—if you could call her a salesperson, and if you could call what she's doing *working*—has her back to me as she reads a magazine. She must be new. I've never seen her here before. I could pocket these glasses and be on my way, and she wouldn't even know it. But shoplifting's not my thing. No, I'll work for whatever I need.

Problem is, a kid has to be sixteen to get a real job, you know, with a paycheck and everything. Those are the rules here in Shunpike Falls. Maybe those are the rules everywhere. I'm not sure. What I *am* painfully sure about is that I just barely turned fifteen, and I haven't had a steady allowance for about a year now.

A few other hard facts come to mind as I slip these wraparound shades on and check out Dachshunda, who's still staring down the south corridor, as if squinting those beady little dachshund eyes and wrinkling her little dachshund snout will produce another electronics store out of thin air.

One: It's early October, and the Queensbury Country Club has just closed down for the season. No more caddying, not that the tightwads up there pay very much.

Two: People in Queensbury and down here in the Falls have started letting their lawns go for the season, so mowing isn't an option either.

Three: The leaves won't die and fall off the trees for another couple of weeks, so there's nothing to rake. Even when the leaves do fall, raking is a one-shot deal: The leaves fall, you rake them, end of story.

Four: The first snow to shovel is probably two months away, bare minimum.

Conclusion: I'll basically be dead of entertainment starvation any day now if I don't get my hands on some more cash.

Dachshunda makes her move for the exit. Still wearing the shades, I take two steps in her direction, just to see if I could swipe these sunglasses if I wanted to. Easy. I stop, though, and rest them on the edge of the pushcart. The girl with the magazine still doesn't seem to notice I'm even here.

I'm telling you: Give me a job like hers, and I'll work my butt off. Of course, that day is a long way away.

~

I lock onto Dachshunda at her car: a hatchback just big enough for Dachshunda, her kid, and his trombone case. While she fidgets in her purse for her keys, I sneak up behind, my head growing light, my vision going fuzzy around the edges.

"*Caveat emptor,*" I whisper hoarsely, my shadow slithering across the pavement.

The woman turns, blinking her eyes.

Blood races through me like cars around a dirt track.

"Stay there, you," she says, sounding like a substitute teacher making a threat but knowing, deep down, that she's lost control of the class. "Don't come any closer—"

"*Caveaaattt . . .*"—I draw the sound out into a long hiss— "*. . . emptor.*" I spit in her direction for effect, surprised at how naturally the gesture comes to me. "*Caveat emptor,*" I repeat in a low, gravelly voice that seems to begin way down in my Chuck Taylors. I step toward her. "*Caveat . . .*"

Something registers in Dachshunda's eyes, and she clutches the collar of her coat around her neck.

"*. . . emptor!*"

"You . . . you, there," she whimpers. "You, stay there."

"*Caveat emptor,*" I chant, now about a yard away from her.

She begins to shake, like a gazelle that has sensed, too late, a cheetah arriving on the scene.

Leaning toward her, I whisper, "*Caveat emptor.*"

She recoils and, in a spasm, empties her purse on the hood of the car. A few things roll off onto the pavement. "T-t-take it," she pleads. "Take it all!"

A wave of confusion jostles me back to reality, my head still spinning. I automatically step back.

"Take it!" Dachshunda shrieks, pushing the wallet away from the rest of the junk on the hood and running around to the rear of her car. "P-p-please, don't hurt me."

Hurt you? The idea freezes me right where I stand.

"Help!" she screams and starts sprinting toward the mall, flailing her arms and legs so violently that she falls

45

down. She gets right up, though—and fast—and keeps on running.

My limbs tingle as I watch her. Looking at the wallet on the hood of the car, I feel queasy. I mean, what does she think I am, some kind of criminal?

"Are you okay?" a man's voice calls in the distance.

"Help!" Dachshunda howls.

I take off.

5

I use my intimate knowledge of the fast-food joints lining Winston Road to stay out of sight as I jog to Legion Park. I started hearing sirens as soon as I split the mall parking lot. I don't know if the cops were responding to Dachshunda's hysterical shrieking, but I'm not taking any chances. As I pass through the greasy back lots, cutting through the foul-smelling secret corridor, some restaurant workers on cigarette breaks give me weird looks. I keep moving, ready to duck behind a dumpster at the first sight of a police cruiser.

Spilling out behind Pizza Hut, I dash across the strip of dead trees bordering one side of the park. About fifty yards away, I spot two familiar forms perched on the small rise of grass and dirt we call the Mound.

"Well?" Page says as I collapse at the foot of the Mound. "You left us hanging back there at the mall. What's the deal?"

I roll onto my back and stare at the sky for a couple of seconds. Two clouds right above me look like they're sumo wrestling. "What's the deal?" I echo Page's question. "That's a good choice of words." I consider my options:

Do I tell my friends what I've just done? They're going to find out sooner or later. Will they think I'm being greedy if I don't include them in this business—a business that looks like it could really take off? Will they think I'm being stupid if I keep on doing it—I mean, stupider than I've already been? Maybe they'd like a piece of the action

. . .

"You're being awfully quiet over there," Marcus says, "especially for the guy who called this meeting."

I take a deep breath. "How you guys doing for money?"

Neither answers right away.

"I get a fairly generous allowance," Marcus says. "You're aware of that, I think."

He's right. I am aware of that. Marcus's family is on the wealthy side, at least by Airport neighborhood standards. His dad transferred from another division of Quadrangle, outside of Boston, to become the number-three guy over in Quarry. He's basically my mother's boss, about five times removed.

"What about you, Page?" I say. "You could use a few bucks, couldn't you?"

"Enough with the questions." She tosses a pebble at me, just missing my head. "What did you do? Did you do something stupid?"

"Tell me you didn't rob somebody," Marcus says, taking his voice way down low, like he sometimes does when he's being ultra-serious.

"No," I say. "I didn't rob anybody. In fact, I gave something back. I gave something back to some people who had it coming. People who like to push other people

48

around. People who don't like kids in torn jeans. I bet they don't like black people either. And I'm guessing they couldn't care less about your little feminist agenda, Page—"

"Watch your tone with me," she snaps. "And it's *not* a 'little' agenda."

"Maybe not," I say, "but let's face it. Does anyone here in Shunpike Falls really care what we think about anything? Does anyone ever listen to our complaints?"

"What exactly are you talking about, Mitch?" Marcus says. "You found a way to air our grievances?"

I roll so I can see his face, just to make sure it's Marcus and not his father sitting there. The way Marcus talks sometimes, it's hard to tell the difference. "That's exactly what I found. But it's not just about airing grievances. There's a little bit of . . ." I scour my brain for that term Framm used in class the other day. He was talking about that dude who went to live by that pond and wrote about it. Henry something. Something about not paying taxes because he didn't believe in it. *Thoreau*—that's it. Henry David Thoreau. *Civil disobedience.*

Before I can say the words, Jimmy charges over the top of the Mound. Page screams, and Marcus and I scramble out of the way as he rolls like a bowling ball between us. When he stops at the bottom of the Mound, he laughs that cartoon-chipmunk laugh that I usually get a kick out of. Usually. The rest of us don't say anything, probably because we're in shock.

"What's cracking, freaks?" Jimmy says, flipping his chin in my direction—the trademark Jimmy Biggins greeting—and ripping another chipmunk laugh into the night.

As he scrambles to his feet and approaches us, however, the group mood on the Mound quickly shifts from heart-attack startled to majorly depressed. I can tell, just from a glance at Marcus and Page, that we've all noticed the same thing: the massive bump on Jimmy's left cheekbone, only partly hidden under his stringy blond hair. Even though we're all used to seeing Jimmy with new bumps and bruises, it's still a total drag. His face and hands are dirty, as if he's been camping out the past couple of nights, which is not unlikely, given how insane things get at the Biggins household.

Jimmy's folks are just plain nasty—drunks and, obviously, rough with their kid. Jimmy's older brother, Shane, dropped out of Shunpike High his sophomore year, and Jimmy hasn't seen or heard from him since. That was a couple years ago now. I can't say that I miss him, Shane. He hung out with some pretty dangerous guys—Kirby Ploof, Buck Twitchell, Randy Martello, and a few other delinquents I'd cross the street to avoid. But sometimes, when Jimmy's in a bad stretch at home, getting beaten a lot, I sort of wish Shane would come back and kick his parents' asses. Then again, it's none of my business. Even Jimmy would tell me that, and he's my oldest friend.

Something about Jimmy's latest shiner tweaks my memory: "Last night," I say before I'm aware of the words forming in my mind.

"What about it?" Jimmy jogs a cigarette out of the pack he picks up off the ground, where it landed after popping out of his pocket.

50

"Valley Road," I say.

Jimmy stares at me through the darkness, then shakes his head.

I exhale with relief. "Do you know who did it?"

He nods.

"Were you there?"

He pauses, then shakes his head again. "Two guys from Quarry. Shane's friends. I was with them just before, smoking a butt at the brickyard."

"Did you tell the cops?"

Jimmy stares at me again, but it's different this time. It's as if he's looking right through me. "What do you think?" he mutters as if it's the stupidest question in the world, which, now that I think about it, it sort of is. "No," he adds. "I didn't tell the cops. That's why I got this." He touches the side of his face with two fingertips. "My folks don't like police cruisers blocking the driveway."

"Dude," Marcus says in the low-serious voice. "Are you okay?"

Jimmy shrugs and blows smoke into the wind. "It ain't your problem."

Marcus looks down at his shoes. "I know, but, still, somebody should say something to them—"

"Why don't you, Marcus, if you're so fricking worried? Huh? You go up there and tell my folks what you think of the way they treat their kid."

"Oh, they'd love that, wouldn't they?" Marcus shakes his head. "I remember how welcome they made me feel the last time I was there. The first *and* last time. I'm surprised they weren't wearing white hoods."

We're all silent for a while as Jimmy smokes, and we

51

just listen to the whine of sirens, the approaching thunder of jets.

"How you doing for money, Jimmy?" I say as a jet starts to drag its noisy net over us.

"Broke. You?"

"Not quite broke. But . . ."

"But what?"

"I do have a plan."

"Wait, let me guess." Jimmy blows smoke at me, but I wave it away. "We go over to Quick Stop, and someone distracts the cash-register guy while we steal the returned bottles out of the back room. Then we bring them down to Penny Pantry and cash them in."

"Infants," Page groans and falls onto her back.

"You're right, Page," I say, shouting a little to compete with the jet drawing closer. "That's kid stuff. I'm talking about civil disobedience."

Marcus nods at me. "Henry David Thoreau."

"Right," I say. "A protest. Rebellion."

"Protest against what?" Page says, sounding very interested now as she props herself up on her elbows.

"Not against what. Against who."

"Against *whom*," Marcus corrects me. That's Marcus: Not even a jet screaming toward us will keep him from correcting my grammar.

"Against whom?" Page shouts.

Marcus and Jimmy lean closer.

"Rude people," I shout back just before we're swallowed in engine roar. "People who don't like us."

Customer Service

6

We cruise the south corridor in a tight pack, watching for any sign of the Ginger, Dachshunda, or the RediGards. Page and Marcus walk up front, with me sort of hidden in the middle, Jimmy bringing up the rear. We're careful not to be distracted and move apart, not even when we pass the atrium, where a guy's demonstrating kitchen knives that cut through copper tubing. Here and there people call out to me—Barb Antell from Fashion Focus, Louise Carruccio from Yarn Barn—but the pack holds together. When we've cruised the mall from one end to the other, I suggest we split up, check in on some of the stores, see if we can offer any "customer service."

"So, am I to assume we're open for business?" Marcus says, a trace of nervousness in his voice.

A film of sweat coats my forehead. "I guess so."

"You *guess* so?" Page says.

This is it. This is the situation that calls for a leader. Pickett's Charge at the Battle of Gettysburg, Ralph in *Lord of the Flies*—a book Framm made us read. The thoughts flip through my head like flashcards. As I stand here, trying to give the command to charge into retail battle, I'm entranced by the people strolling by. They seem to move in slow motion, plodding along with heavy steps, as if trudging through manure. Catching me staring, a few shoppers stare back, their shopping-crazed eyes burning into my light head.

Jimmy lets out a chipmunk chuckle, and I turn to my friends.

I'm startled to see Marcus wearing a plastic Hello Kitty mask. As my jaw drops open, he tilts the mask back onto his head: "I've got an easy face to remember around here."

"That's a great idea," I say.

"Hours o' Wonder." Marcus nods in the direction of the toy and hobby store down near Big Buy. He takes the mask off and snaps its rubber-band strap before sticking it inside his shirt. "Eight bucks."

"I'm getting one too," Jimmy says. "Someone loan me eight bucks."

"I'll front you," I say and slip Jimmy an Alex H. "We should all get them." I glance down the corridor toward Hours o' Wonder. "*Caveat emptor.* Everybody got it?"

"*Caveat emptor,*" Page says.

"*Caveat emptor,*" Marcus echoes.

Jimmy looks down at his well-scuffed black boots—the same kind Shane Biggins used to wear.

"Jimmy," I say.

"Cavity . . ."

"*Cah-vee-yat . . . ,*" I correct him.

"*Cavity . . . emptoh . . .*"

"*Caveat emptor—*"

"I've fricking got it, okay? The frick's it mean, anyway?"

I hesitate, realizing that even I still don't know.

"It's Latin," Marcus says. "It means, 'Let the buyer beware.'"

"'Let the buyer beware,'" I repeat, feeling my biological war drum start pounding out a rhythm in my chest.

"Whatever," Jimmy sneers. "They'll get the idea."

A breeze carrying the faint essence of floor wax washes over me just as I spot Brian Bigelow gesturing from His New Look. "Meet at the Mound after," I say.

~

Brian's working on what some Onion River Mall salespeople call a Mentor: any adult male who's incapable of interacting with a kid without dispensing as much useless advice as he can possibly get out of his big mouth. I generally find Mentors harmless—incredibly annoying, but harmless.

So I guess I'm not exactly looking forward to hitting this particular Mentor: a tall, rangy guy with receding, gray-blond hair gathered in a ponytail roughly the size of a rabbit's foot. I'm just not feeling the urge to take him down, not just yet. As I wait by the racks of leather jackets at the front of the store, I try to think bad thoughts. Fortunately, the sound of the man's voice helps me get there. He's not talking to Brian—he's *lecturing*:

"You see, that's just the problem with your generation," he declares from in front of a full-length mirror, where he strokes the baby blue sweater vest he wears over a tan chamois shirt. "Well, let *me* tell *you*, when *I* was *your* age . . ."

~

"When I was your age . . . When I was your age . . . When I was your age . . ."

I let the words ring in my ears. Among all the adult phrases that make me want to shove someone off the Onion River Bridge, this one's at the top of the list.

~

With another Hamilton crammed into my pocket, I track the Mentor down the south corridor and out the southwest exit. Trailing him into the lot, I stick close to the building, hidden in the contours of the loading docks jutting out. I catch my larger-than-life reflection against the wall: a killer, an assassin, a hit man.

Stepping out of the shadows and slipping unnoticed into a row of cars, I'm relieved to discover that the Mentor has parked his metallic blue SUV, with its torpedo-shaped roof rack, close to the trees separating the mall parking lot from the bank. Directly beyond the SUV I spot a thinning row of bushes that looks perfect for a getaway.

The chirp of the car alarm startles me as I sneak up behind the Mentor and pull on my Hello Kitty mask. He turns.

"*Caveat emptor,*" I say and point at him, my fingers forming two imaginary pistols.

"What?"

"*Caveat emptor.*" I walk toward him, not stopping until my face is about two feet away from his. "*Caveat emptor.*"

The guy looks more confused than frightened as he checks out my mask.

The longer he inspects me, the harder I focus on the way

he lectured Brian, ran him around the store, then left without a "thank you"—just a pile of cheesy vests to straighten up and put back. And those magic words: "When I was your age . . ."

"Caveat emptor," I repeat, not particularly impressed with the power of my voice.

When the Mentor smirks and folds his arms across his chest, I almost turn and run. "Beware of *what,* smart guy?" he says.

I clench my fists as a bead of sweat trickles under the mask's elastic band. Glancing quickly at the SUV, I see a bumper sticker that reads, SUPPORT SHUNPIKE FALLS YOUTH SOCCER—IT'S A KICK IN THE GRASS.

"Caveat emptor," I repeat, my voice dropping a few notes as I step back and begin bouncing on the balls of my feet. I kick at the space between us a couple of times— half-karate kicks, as if I'm just warming up for the butt-whupping about to ensue. *"Caveat . . ."* Bounce, bounce, bounce. *". . . emptor!"* Kick! *"Caveat . . ."* Bounce, bounce, bounce. *". . . emptor!"* Kick!

The second time I kick at the air, the Mentor flinches and shifts his weight from one foot to the other.

"Caveat . . ." I have absolutely no idea why I'm doing what I'm doing, but I bow at the waist, as if our little ninja match will now begin for real. *". . . emptor."*

The Mentor takes a half-step back and unfolds his arms, a frown replacing his smug, defiant expression.

"Caveat emptor," I say with a weird, hyena-like laugh I don't think I've ever produced before. I advance two steps closer.

The Mentor frowns, and a little curtain of hair slips

from his ponytail scrunchie and falls down over his wrinkled brow. "What is this all about?" he asks, his voice cracking faintly.

"*Caveat . . . ,*" I growl like my gym teacher, Mr. McQuay, and chop at the air directly in front of the Mentor's face, "*. . . emptor!*"

The man's eyes flash with alarm as he raises his hands in front of his face. "Please, I, I . . . ," he pleads, "I'll give you whatever you want—my wallet. Let me get—"

"*Caveat emptor,*" I not so much say as proclaim and laugh again—this time a sinister, mad-scientist's laugh. I seem to have no control over my voice or actions. My own twisted imagination is completely in charge.

The Mentor backs away and slinks around the front of the SUV. As I tail him, he lets out a faint whine.

"*Caveat emptor,*" I whisper in his ear, breath puffing out the sides of my mask like dragon smoke.

"Help!" he screams. Turning to run, he collides with the SUV parked next to his. His knees hit the car with a nasty crunch.

"Help! Security!" he shouts, hobbling away.

Walking as calmly as I can toward my escape hatch in the woods, my sweatshirt flaps in the breeze. My shadow grows wings, and I fly away.

7

I have to admit, I actually enjoy being at school these days. Even though there's not much to spend money on here, except maybe drugs or a gun or a knife or something, none of which I have much use for, I just like knowing that I've got a little cash in my pocket—thanks to a couple more busy nights at the Onion River Mall for Jimmy, Marcus, Page, and me. Theoretically, if there were anything to buy at Shunpike High that I actually wanted, which there isn't, except for food from the à la carte line in the cafeteria, I could buy it. And that's a very good feeling. Yes, I believe I could get used to that.

In fact, I've already decided to treat myself to whatever looks good on the à la carte line. That's why I'm standing here, waiting for the line to snake its way into the kitchen. Based on what kids are bringing out the other side, it looks like I'll have my choice of pizza and pizza rolls, cheeseburgers, onion rings—basically, the stuff I'd eat every single meal, every single day, if I could afford to. Today I can, so I will.

Some Laurel Heights dude who's dressed almost as preppily as Marcus gives me the stink-eye when I check out his tray: a pizza roll, fries, two chocolate milks. I know it's impolite to watch other people eat, but I've never ordered from this line before. I can't help staring.

See, the two cafeteria lunchrooms at Shunpike High work out to be smaller versions of Shunpike Falls: Airport kids over on the other side, with our government ketchup, government soy burgers, and governmentally dehydrated then rehydrated mashed potatoes; Laurel Heights kids over here, with all the edible food. But this isn't a rule. In theory, any kid can get his food in whichever line he wants—so long as he can pay for it. He can also eat in whichever lunchroom he wants to. In theory.

In practice, what you eat for lunch ends up being just another way of defining who you are and who you aren't, where you live and where you don't, what you have and what you have to verbally attack people in a mall parking lot to get.

I try to focus on something else as the line moves ahead a few feet. That's when I notice Keith Sullivan duck into the lunchroom from the hallway. He's impossible to miss as he slaloms around the tables. In about three of his giraffe strides he's standing right next to me.

Another second later, he's wrapping one long arm around my shoulder and pressing a shoebox to my chest with the other. "A token of my appreciation, yo," he says from atop his tower of wiry muscle.

I lift the box lid. Inside is a brand-new pair of gleaming, black leather Kourt Kingz. "Keith, man," I say, "I can't take—"

"No worries, Mitch. They're red-tags. Got a factory defect. Can't sell them."

"You should give these to Jimmy. I mean, he did the hit

for you." Last night at Off the Bench Sports, the king of all couch-potato pro sports fans suckered Keith into a debate about the history of college basketball over the past one thousand years. According to Jimmy, the customer tried on nearly every "official" college basketball jersey in the store—and Off the Bench Sports has tons of them—but said he wouldn't buy one unless Keith could pass a little quiz. I guess Keith didn't pass. So he had Jimmy administer a little Latin quiz of his own in the parking lot.

"Already spoke to the J-man," Keith says. "These shoes don't fit him. He's going to stop by the store later this week, and we'll let him pick out something special."

I eye the shoes lying in the box like sleeping puppies. They're my size, I can tell at a glance. Still, the prospect of owning them doesn't seem real. "Keith," I say, "I don't know what to say. Thank—"

"You don't have to say anything, Mitch. Or, that is, you don't have to say anything . . . to *me*." He slaps me on the back—a gentle slap, fortunately. "Just make sure your gang keeps sticking it to my nasty customers." He glides back across the cafeteria and out into the hall, his head floating above the students like a toy boat on a stream.

Gang. Is that what we are?

A tingle crawls down my neck.

I'm suddenly less interested in pizza rolls than in talking business with Page, Marcus, and Jimmy. I mean, a *gang*? I never intended for us to become a . . . *gang*.

I look at the Kourt Kingz again. I'd have to verbally assault half of Shunpike Falls out in the parking lot of the

Onion River Mall to afford a pair of these sneakers. But here they are, in my hands, soon to be on my feet.

Caveat emptor. Two little Latin words, and I can have things I once only dreamed of: phat sneakers, a pizza roll for lunch, popularity. Two little Latin words. Too bad the school cut Latin last spring. Turns out it's actually a very useful language.

Someone passing behind me says, "The Mall Mafia—no fear!"

I turn around and find a table of freshman guys raising their fists in salute. *Mall Mafia,* I think as I nod back. *That's a new one.*

A little freaked out, I cross back to the Airport side of the cafeteria, get my usual government-subsidized lunch, and sit down alone. I set the shoebox in front of my tray but leave the lid on. I take a few bites of soy burger and look around. Kids I've never noticed before in my life nod and wave. After a couple more bites, I break down and take out the Kingz.

Marcus and Page show up just as I'm lacing the second sneaker. "Nice wheels," Page says. "You win the lottery?"

"No. Keith Sullivan gave them to me. 'A token of his appreciation.'"

"Graft's more like it," Marcus says.

"He claims they were red-tags. I think the defect is in the stitching here along the tongue." I run a finger along the left shoe. The shoes fit like a second layer of skin. I feel like I could jam a basketball with these things on, which, of course, is ridiculous, given my height issues.

"What a coincidence," Page says. "I ran into Theresa

Wright down in front of the library two periods ago. Now, Theresa the Terrible and I have never exchanged more than five words."

"I think she only knows four," Marcus says. *"Boy. Hate. Penis. Bad."*

"Yeah, well, she walked right up to me and said, 'Page, I just want to say that you're an inspiration to militant feminists everywhere.'"

"Is that a compliment?" I say.

Page scowls at me. "Then I remembered that she's Mavis Carter's best friend. Mavis Carter from the Bath and Beauty Bar, where I helped her with that snobby yuppie woman, the one with the electric tan and the stick up her—"

"I thought you didn't like Theresa," Marcus says.

"I don't like her politics, but, I'll admit, I was a tiny bit flattered."

Marcus pulls his chair up closer to the table. "Speaking of flattery, check this out. Just before fourth period, I walked right past three of those Next of Skin cretins . . . and not one racial slur. Not one. I wanted to hug them."

"That might be pushing it," I say and stand up on my new shoes. Marcus and Page watch as I check them out from a few different angles.

Something out in the hallway catches Page's attention. "No, I'll tell you what's pushing it," she says as Jimmy walks past the cafeteria door with Harry Williams and Kyle Lindberg, two burnouts from the junior class. I have a pretty good idea where they're headed: the kickboard.

In an incredibly stupid bit of planning, school

administrators placed a kickboard roughly the size of a soccer goal up against the woods at the far end of the soccer field. This means that anyone behind the kickboard is invisible from the school building. The world's greatest architects couldn't have designed a better place to get baked between periods.

"Looks like Jimmy's got some new friends," Page mutters.

"I saw him regaling Harry and Kyle and a bunch of other derelicts with tales of his mall exploits," Marcus says, "how he basically chased that guy's car out of the parking lot, banging on the glass. They found it very amusing, to say the least."

"I can't believe how fast word has spread about this whole mall deal," I say, sitting back down. "The Mall Mafia. That's what they're calling us."

Marcus nods. "You hit a nerve, Mitch. You were in the right place at the right time." He's using his lawyer voice now, which makes him seem like a know-it-all. Of his many voices, it's my least favorite.

"What do you mean, 'hit a nerve'?" I say. "And stop talking like that."

"What I mean," he says more like my friend than my attorney, "is that we may be looking at the start of a bona fide trend."

"Explain that," Page says, her eyebrows wrinkled like two pieces of black yarn.

Marcus taps a finger on the table. "Think about it. No matter how unpleasant it may be to work at the mall, do we honestly think it's bad enough to justify the payback customers get from this mysterious Mall Mafia? Don't get me wrong, I'm not complaining. I realize we get paid for that payback."

Page and I look at each other.

"Or maybe it *is* bad enough," Marcus continues with a shrug. "But maybe it's also becoming . . . let's say . . . *cool* to do business with a certain group of sharp-tongued sophomores."

"Cool?" I say, trying to equate that value—the ultimate characteristic, the most desirable quality, the "zenith," as Mr. Framm might call it, of social status—with something I did. I can't. I mean, Keith Sullivan is cool: He's seven feet tall and scores whenever he wants to. Tammy Bernard's cool: Her teeth are so white she can jog at night without wearing reflective clothing. A tattoo of your girlfriend's name on your biceps is cool (so long as you have a girlfriend and a biceps big enough for her name, neither of which I do). Going somewhere sunny and warm over spring break is cool. (I usually stay home and get caught up on my late-night TV.) Supermodels, pro athletes, rock stars, and certain TV actors are cool. Paying me ten bucks to harass a mall shopper in Latin . . . That's cool?

"That's crazy," I say. "That makes absolutely no sense."

"Who said it makes sense?" Marcus pauses as if to let his idea sink in to my inferior brain. "Since when has any of this . . ." He gestures with a sweep of his arm around the cafeteria just as a lump of mashed potatoes arcs through the air from one table and lands on another directly beside ours.

A high-pitched shriek cuts through the rumble of voices as a girl in a nuclear-green miniskirt walks by, a matching cell phone pressed to her head: "Omigod! I'm, like, no way!"

Two dudes wearing tattered baseball caps trade shoulder punches, laughing one moment, grimacing the next, laughing one moment, grimacing the next.

A girl in wraparound sunglasses carves an intricately detailed American flag in a cafeteria tray, singing along to the music pounding so loudly from her headphones that I could name the song from here.

My eye drifts down to my new sneakers. They're so shiny they practically glow, like coals in a barbecue grill.

When I look up again, Marcus is smiling and shaking his head. "Since when has any of this *ever* made sense?"

8

Page, Marcus, and I have been waiting for Jimmy on the edge of the woods behind the mall for almost an hour. Dusk is settling in, which suits our purpose, but Jimmy's still not here, which doesn't suit our purpose. We all agreed—Jimmy included—that we'd meet here and plan our strategy before working the mall. Demand for our services has been overwhelming, so it seemed like a good idea to think things through a little bit, just to keep this business from spiraling out of control.

The problem is, Jimmy doesn't handle orders too well—not even very mellow orders. By now he's been breaking rules for so long he's practically programmed himself to do exactly the opposite of what anyone tells him to.

Finally, the exit door flies open and Jimmy struts out. He stands in place, looking around as if trying to remember why he came outside in the first place, then lights a cigarette.

I step out of the weeds, Page and Marcus following. "What's the deal, Jimmy?" I say. "We've been waiting for you—"

"Relax, freaks," he says with a cheesy grin and a flip of his chin. "I was just playing video games. Made fourth-highest score on Commando Zone. Cost me just about six bucks, but, hey, there's plenty more where that came from."

"My hero," Page mutters.

Jimmy narrows his eyes at her and picks tobacco off his tongue. "So, is this what we're going to do, stand around like a bunch of chicks—"

"Watch it," Page says.

". . . or are we going to begin the beatdown?" Jimmy blows a puff of smoke at me. "You're kind of amped today. You aren't wussing out, are you—"

"From now on, when we say we're going to meet in a certain place, at a certain time, be there."

"Aw, Mitch," he sneers. "Listen to you. Like somebody's fricking Cub Scout leader."

"Call me what you want, Jimmy, but if we don't stay organized, we're going to get nailed."

"Do I look scared? As my dad might say, this is like shooting fish in a barrel."

"Now *there's* a sportsman for you," Page mutters.

Jimmy flicks his cigarette past her, close enough for her to flinch. "So, are we psyched or what?" he says, his cold brown eyes fixed on me.

"We're not psyched to get caught," I say, starting toward the mall entrance. "Try to remember that. I'm going to talk to the Chair. Meet at the Mound in an hour."

"Whatever," Jimmy says, with a trace of that chipmunk laugh.

∼

The Chair stands midway down the store, straightening the remains of the summer clearance rack. "Would you

69

just look at this," he groans, his gray-wool arms outstretched. "They've completely casseroled this whole display."

The rack is essentially a pile of shoes in no apparent order. Even the "End-of-Summer Sensations!" sign hanging over the rack looks a bit tattered and crooked. "Yeah, it's a mess—"

"Savages. No respect for the rules of decent human conduct."

"Speaking of rules," I say, "I notice more than the usual number of security officers on duty tonight. Or am I just paranoid?"

"What do you have to be paranoid about?"

"Well, Lance and the RediGards haven't, like, asked you anything, you know, about . . . the woman?"

The Chair stops tidying. "The woman?"

"The Ginger."

"Ah, yes. The Ginger. Did you do the job?"

"Is a frog's butt waterproof?"

"Very mature, Mitch. Very mature." The Chair glances around the store, as if suddenly worried about being seen with me. "And I understand you've had other clients in the meantime."

"Word travels fast around this place."

"I guess so. Burke's the only person I told."

Sheila Burke is one of the Chair's employees, and she's a junior at Shunpike High. "Let's just hope nobody tells Lance," I add.

The Chair glances around again, then gestures to the stockroom. "Step in back for a second."

I follow him into the stockroom and climb a few rungs

of a sliding ladder leaning out from the floor-to-ceiling shelves. While he disappears down one aisle of shoeboxes, I think back to the all-too-brief period when I worked here. I'd memorized where every style of shoe, every stock number, fit into these walls. Tell me you want a navy blue espadrille in a size seven—bingo, I'd have it for you in seconds. And I'd yank down the half-sizes smaller and larger, just to save you another trip. But thanks to Gladys the Chin, those days are over.

"*Caveat emptor,*" I say as the Chair returns with a stack of papers under his arm.

He leans against the shoebox wall across from me. "Yeah, *caveat emptor.*" He begins shuffling through his papers—spreadsheets, most likely. That's the thing about the Chair: He almost never gives you his full attention. Even when I was working back here, when I was supposed to be *helping* him out, he sat at his desk reading *Playboy* while I climbed around this dusty tomb like a lemur on Ritalin. "It's Latin," I say. "'Let the buyer beware.'"

"You're right. Smart kid."

"Marcus told me. It really freaks these people out."

"That was the general idea."

The Chair tries to go back to reading his spreadsheets, but I distract him by rhythmically shaking the ladder on its runner, making what must be an annoying sound. At least that's what the look on his face says. "You okay?" he asks. "Was there some problem with the job?"

"The Ginger? No. No problem."

"Then what is it? You're all, like, tweaky."

"What . . . what are we doing, Chair?"

71

"You mean you and your little gang, there?"

The word *gang* sends a tingle down my neck. "My friends and I. I just want to make sure that this isn't totally stupid. Because it seems things could get out of control."

"How so?"

"*Everybody* at the mall wants our business."

"Well, that's good, right?"

I start to answer but hesitate. I launched this venture to make money, and that's what it's doing, but there's also something about it that makes me very uncomfortable: the prospect of getting caught.

"And, frankly," the Chair continues, "I'm not at all surprised that there's demand out there for the service you provide. I get *tremendous* satisfaction knowing you knocked that Ginger down a few pegs. A lot of the salespeople here in the mall must feel the same way."

"Tell me, though, isn't there something just a little weird about this service I provide?"

The Chair actually seems to contemplate the question as he stops riffling his papers and gazes up at a flickering fluorescent ceiling light. Eventually, he rolls his papers up in one hand and smacks the shoebox wall behind him, producing an impressive cloud of dust. He gives me a serious look. "Yes. Yes, this is a very weird thing you're doing. And, sure, there are risks. You might get caught. You might meet up with someone with the guts to defend himself. And you'll definitely piss people off. But nothing ventured, nothing gained, right? No guts, no glory. Kill or be killed. 'Insult or be insulted.' Wasn't that what you said? Or do you mean to tell me that these pathetic insecurities were running through your head when you hit that Ginger? Were they?"

Caught off-guard by his sudden change of mood, I don't respond right away.

"No, they weren't," he answers for me. "I'll tell you why. Because at the end of the day, a kid—*especially* a kid your age—can use a little cash. Am I right?"

"Of course," I say, looking at him, "but it also feels a little . . . I don't know . . . wrong."

"Does it, now? Does it really feel that way?"

I want to say yes, but the word sticks in my throat. The truth is, it feels wrong only when I think about it, mainly because I know it's *supposed* to feel wrong. When I was right in the middle of the Ginger, Dachshunda, and Mentor hits, it felt good . . . in a weird way. It felt good to give a little back to those crabby bastards.

The Chair nods, as if pleased with himself for knowing what I'm thinking, then gives the wall another whack with his paper club. "You've got it," he says.

"Got what?"

"A chip on your shoulder, a sense for when people are getting dumped on. Like I'm sure you sometimes get dumped on—"

"*I* don't get dumped on," I interrupt.

He gives me an "Are you kidding me?" look that makes me squirm on the ladder.

"No, of course you don't," he says in a tone that tells me I'm not fooling him, not for a nanosecond—as if anyone ever could. "But nonetheless, Mitch, you put yourself in my shoes, and you saw what I needed—to get back at

73

that woman. You could do that because you too need to get back at something. Someone."

I peer up the wall of shoeboxes.

He kicks the ladder so that I'll turn my attention back to him. That's another thing about the Chair: While he reserves the right to ignore everyone, he refuses to be ignored.

"What?"

"No, Mitch. Who. The old man. Why are you so yanked at the guy?"

A flash of blood heats up my face, as if the Chair's just lit some fuse I've been trying to keep hidden. He's definitely found it. And I know he knows he's found it.

"He's not kicking in hard with the allowance, is he, Mitch?"

I look away. The Chair lets me ignore him for a few seconds, but I know it won't last for long.

"Sorry. I didn't mean to bring up a sensitive subject—"

"It's not a sensitive subject," I say.

The Chair gives me that older-brother look, the one that says, "You actually expect me to believe that?" He goes back to flipping through his spreadsheets. "But be honest," he says, "the old man would *not* be psyched about this mall . . . business."

My heart starts racing.

The Chair shakes his head. "No. He's not exactly a big fan of the Onion River Mall—"

"Let's not get into that."

"Whatever you say, Mitch." As the Chair ambles up the aisle, pushing boxes in here and there, my mind floods

74

with the memory of Dad's one-man picket line at the mall's grand opening, captured for eternity by Mrs. Pegg's camera for the *Beacon:*

Developer Stages Solo Mall Protest
Reginald Grant Fired for Challenging Onion River Deal
Firm Threatens Lawsuit

"He should just go back there and beg," I say.

"The real estate firm?" The Chair looks at me from down the aisle.

"Yeah." I stare at the floor. "He's not in great shape these days."

"I know." The Chair walks back to my perch. "I've heard." The Chair leans on my ladder and gives me that older-brother look again. "I'm going to tell you something important," he says. "I'm telling you this because I don't think anyone ever has. Someone should."

He paces a few yards down the aisle, stops, and punches a shoebox sticking out from the wall. "In life . . . you don't get what you deserve." He points at me. "You get what you negotiate for. Remember that." He looks up at the fluorescent light again, watches it flicker. "It's not the nicest way to think, I'll admit, but for now let's just call it a necessary evil."

I don't like the sound of that last word, but the Chair starts for the sales floor before I can say anything.

A couple of seconds later, Sheila Burke walks into the stockroom, lets out a little groan, and starts looking around, her red ponytail swinging this way and that. She's startled when she finds me sitting up here on the ladder. "There you are," she says and reaches into the pocket of her pin-striped suit pants. "I've got a Ginger who needs some attitude adjustment. Can you handle her?"

I tap my sweatshirt to make sure my Hello Kitty mask is still tucked in there. Tracing its plastic form starts the internal war drums. "Sure," I say, descending the ladder.

"Can you break a fifty?"

"Uh . . . as a matter of fact, I can."

9

"And then . . . then . . . when I repeated it . . ." Jimmy's choking the words out through cartoon-chipmunk laughter as he stands on top of the Mound. ". . . the guy comes at me like this." He puts his Hello Kitty mask on and rips down the hill. "*Aaargh!*" he growls, hands out in front, staggering toward Marcus like a wolfman.

Marcus ducks out of the way, and Jimmy falls in a chipmunk-laughing heap on the grass.

"He what?" I say.

"Yeah. Charged right fricking at me," Jimmy says, taking his mask off and tossing it onto the grass. "So I kicked him. See if he goes shopping for basketball shoes anytime soon." He sits up and jogs a cigarette out of the pack.

"You did *what?*" My stomach tightens as the image of an old man hooked up to hospital equipment pops into my mind: *Valley Road.*

"And I ran straight up onto the hood of his car—a pretty nice rig, too." Jimmy blows smoke into the breeze and lets out another chipmunk laugh. "An old Mazda or something. I ran right up over the top and into the trees."

"Wait. You mean you really kicked this guy, as in, like, with your foot?"

Jimmy shrugs. "One little one. He fricking asked for it."

"But that's going a little far, don't you think?"

"Self-fricking-defense, Mitch."

I feel another squeeze in my gut. "Hold on. I mean, that's not really what we're hired to do—"

"What difference does it make?" Jimmy cuts me off. "So what about you guys? How'd your hits go down?"

Feeling queasy all of a sudden, I stare across the park, zoning out. I listen vaguely to Page's and Marcus's reports. She freaked out some crewcut hard-ass who'd reprimanded Brenda Allen in front of a store full of Kitchens Inc. customers that she didn't know "a blessed thing" about housewares. Then he grilled her with questions about stuff like how often a bread knife should be sharpened, what the preferred method for cleaning automatic-drip coffee makers is, and so on. Page says the guy acted so shocked when she cornered him in the lot that maybe she's the first person to stand up to him in his life— "And a woman, no less!"

Marcus's hit was a crazed knitter who'd been hassling Louise Carruccio at Yarn Barn. The woman shrieked like an opera singer, is how Marcus puts it, as he chased her around her car.

"Sounds like everything went according to plan," I say weakly, trying to remember exactly what Sheila Burke's Ginger did to make her so mad—and to make me hunt the lady down like a rabid animal. My memory of the hit is already as fuzzy as a scrambled TV channel.

Page is studying me. "What about you, Mitch?" she says. "Any problems with your . . . encounter?"

"No. No big deal. Ginger with a bad attitude."

Jimmy laughs. "Damn," he says, staring up at the sky. "Too bad we can't hustle back over there and fire off another round—"

"Well, we can't," I snap.

The others look at me.

"We can't be stupid about this."

"Easy, Mitch," Marcus says.

The blood rushes to my face as a jet approaches. Despite the chill in the air, I'm sweating. "I don't know," I say, "something's not right about this."

"Something's not right about a lot of things," Page says flatly, almost to herself. "But I did something the past few nights I never thought I could do. I fought back a little."

"Took a walk on the edge," Marcus says. He and Page look at each other and nod.

No one tries to talk as the jet passes overhead. When the roar has faded, Page picks a leaf off her jacket, walks down the Mound, and places it on my shoulder. "A medal for your leadership," she says, then begins walking away.

"Hold up, Page," Marcus says. "I'll walk you home. What about tomorrow night, Mitch?"

"What the frick do you mean?" Jimmy scrambles up off the ground. "Tomorrow night's another beatdown. Right?"

As Marcus and Page drift away from the Mound, everyone looks at me.

"Let's talk in school," I say with what feels like my last breath. "At lunch or something."

"Talk all you want," Jimmy says as he heads toward the

Winston Road strip—in the exact opposite direction of home. "Tomorrow night I'm going back to work."

I roll onto my back and stare into the sky. Gray, fist-shaped clouds scurry across the gunmetal black, as if desperate to get out of Shunpike Falls.

10

I'm disturbed by the look on Vice Principal Decker's face as he watches me through the bullet-proof window of the school office. Seeing me enter the lobby, he says something to his assistant, Mrs. Blodgett. Next to head custodian Mr. Girabaldi, she's Shunpike High's second oldest employee—and the only one with hair dyed the color of an overripe tangerine. Whatever Decker says makes her get up, take a piece of paper from her desk, and walk to the door opening into the lobby. She times her steps so that I'm in direct view when she looks out.

"Mitch Grant," she chirps, flapping the piece of paper in her hand. "Be a dear and post this for me, will you?"

Through the door, which she holds ajar with one knobby calf, I can see Decker still watching me. Out of respect, I'd never refuse Mrs. Blodgett a favor, but the way Decker eyes me over the dark rims of his glasses tells me I don't really have a choice.

"Sure, Mrs. Blodgett," I say, taking the sheet.

She smiles the smile of a rookie spy.

I walk the piece of paper up to the "Community Events" bulletin board. I may be only a sophomore, but

I'm not stupid enough to miss the point of this exercise: to make sure I read the bulletin.

I rearrange the field hockey schedule and a flyer about a French Club–sponsored car wash, then tack up the notice:

PTA Meeting
Tuesday, October 18
Student Activity Center
7 P.M.

Agenda Items:
Teacher Contract Renewal Proposal
New State Math Testing Requirements
The Onion River Mall: "Beware" of What?

I know Decker's watching me, so I pretend not to read the flyer. As I walk away, I crunch some numbers in my head: I've carried out eight hits at the mall so far, and there have been six more each between Jimmy, Marcus, and Page. That's twenty-six attacks total.

Man. Has it been that many?

Except for Jimmy's little act of "self-fricking-defense" last night, I don't know that the Mall Mafia has done anything wrong, necessarily. I mean, we definitely haven't done anything *right*, but I don't think it's *illegal*. Then again, I haven't checked on that yet. I keep meaning to. I guess I've been more focused on the money—more money than I've ever had, even back when my folks could afford to give me an allowance.

Evidently the Shunpike Falls High School parents have decided to look into the Onion River Mall matter themselves. And that makes my own research irrelevant. Because if the PTA is wigged enough by what's going on at the mall to put it on their agenda, then the Mall Mafia is finished. To keep going would be suicide.

And if I read this little "Be a dear and post this for me" drill accurately, Decker knows I'm involved. I mean, isn't that a vice principal's job, to infiltrate the student society and figure out what we're doing? Maybe he's about to share that intelligence with the PTA. If so, that means other parents will soon know what's going on, and word will reach my mother, adding stress to her life that she doesn't need. Or, equally unpleasant, someone will say something to my father, which will add stress to *my* life that *I* don't need.

No. It's definitely over.

I see just one problem in shutting down the operation: Jimmy.

I still have fifteen minutes before the first-period bell, so I head for his favorite hangout: the kickboard.

～

Sure enough, he's back there smoking a butt and talking to Harry Williams, Kyle Lindberg, and a girl named Penny Benoit. Penny's a junior, I think, even though she seems about thirty years old. You could stage an entire school play with the makeup she wears on any given morning.

"Jimmy," I say, hovering at the corner of the kickboard, "I need to talk to you."

"No problem. Come back here."

"Yeah, cutie," Penny says in her husky voice and blows smoke in my direction, "no one's going to hurt you."

"I need to speak to you in private," I say, taking a

tentative step behind the wooden boards, which manage to contain the stale smell of cigarette smoke amazingly well, filtering out all traces of nature and fresh air.

Jimmy shoots me a look that says I'm embarrassing him.

I don't care. "It's important, dude," I say.

"Sounds personal," Penny says with a deep-throated laugh. "Better go, Jimmy. I think he's breaking up with you."

Kyle and Harry think this is about the funniest thing they've ever heard, which it might be to someone who's smoked a pound of weed before the first-period bell. While they're laughing and coughing their lungs out, I get Jimmy to follow me onto the soccer field.

"The hell you doing, freak?" he says when we're out of earshot of the others. "You're making me look like a dork."

"The mall," I say. "We have to quit."

Jimmy stops in his tracks. "The frick you talking about?"

"I saw a notice on the school bulletin board. The PTA's going to discuss our mall . . . activity . . . at their meeting tonight. They know what's been going on."

Jimmy looks at me as if expecting more information. "So?"

"So? So, that means we might get caught."

Jimmy shrugs. "And? You want to quit just because we *might* get caught? I've been caught before. It's no big deal. Dude, I've been caught for things I didn't even *do*."

I look at Jimmy, suddenly feeling like the kid I grew up with is no longer here. There's a tone in his voice that I've

84

never heard before, as though he accepts the way things are and everything people say about him.

"But you don't *want* to get caught, do you?" I ask.

Again, the shrug. "I guess not. But I need the money, you know?"

"You should quit smoking," I say without thinking about it. "You could save money that way." The second the words leave my mouth, I can tell how stupid they sound, how childish.

"Aw, man," Jimmy says with a shake of his head. "You just don't get it, do you?"

"What don't I get?"

Jimmy doesn't say anything for a long time as he looks toward the school, squinting as if we're aboard a ship packed in fog and he's trying to see where we're going. After a while, he pulls some gum wrappers from his pocket and tosses them into the breeze. "We don't live in the same world," he says. "Haven't you figured that out yet?"

I start to answer but hesitate. He's right: Despite the stresses of my home life, I actually *have* one. I wouldn't call what happens at the Biggins house a life. And while I'm sure Decker and the faculty don't expect me to become president of the United States, they probably expect only the worst from Jimmy. Right now, right this moment, he seems determined not to disappoint them.

I want to tell him it doesn't have to be this way, that he can turn things around and show people he's not a delinquent, but who am I to talk? I mean, this whole mall thing was *my* idea.

Jimmy spits on the cold ground, which was covered with frost a couple of hours ago—the first frost of the season. Early frost. "It was Randy Martello and Kirby Ploof," he says.

I look at him, unsure of what he's talking about.

"Valley Road," he adds.

"Why are you telling me this?"

He shrugs again. "I figure at least one person should know the truth, not that it makes any difference."

"I know those guys—I mean, I know who they are."

"Too bad for you. They're fricking tweaked. You'd have to be. I mean, they mugged an old man, Mitch."

"I knew it wasn't you."

Jimmy looks at me for a second, then looks back toward the kickboard. "I hate those guys."

"Then why do you hang out with them?"

"I don't, really. I told you the other night, they were Shane's friends." Jimmy turns away and gets out his cigarettes.

"Better not light that," I say and gesture in the direction of the school building, where Decker's unmistakable form fills the doorway to the Foreign Languages hall. "We're on school property, and Decker's watching."

"He can go to hell," Jimmy says as he sticks a cigarette in his mouth and lights it. At almost the exact instant Jimmy's lighter ignites, Decker starts walking toward us.

"Oh, great," I say.

"Anyway . . ." Jimmy exhales in the crisp morning air, as if the vice principal is completely invisible. ". . . they expect me to hang with them once in a while, Shane's friends. And I guess I kind of feel a connection to Shane when they're around. It's stupid, but . . . You know what I'm saying?"

I nod. "Still, you should avoid being associated with them if you can. They're bad news. Everybody knows it."

Jimmy takes another long drag on his cigarette, his eyes fixed on Decker. "What difference does it make if I associate with them?" he mutters in a cloud of smoke. "I'm one of them, whether I like it or not."

"Mr. Grant! Mr. Biggins!" Decker shouts from about fifty yards away. "Top of the morning to you!"

I automatically take a few steps toward the vice principal. "I was just heading inside, Mr. Decker," I say, my voice sounding higher pitched than I'd intended.

"See you 'round, Mitch," Jimmy says, sounding already far away.

I turn to watch him walk in the other direction, toward the woods.

"Not joining us today, Mr. Biggins?" Decker calls after him.

Jimmy doesn't answer.

As I pass Decker, he mutters in a sarcastic tone you don't often hear from an adult, much less a vice principal, "Well, isn't that just a crying shame?"

11

"I've got a bad feeling about this," Marcus says, "and remember, I'm *used* to being watched."

As Marcus, Page, and I sit by the atrium fountain, it seems like the RediGard security team has doubled overnight. Stu seems especially interested in us, hovering just inside the Joker's Den, monitoring us from behind a rack of cheesy gags—fake hurl and dog crap, those remote control fart machines, and whatnot. I've got to admit, it's funny that Stu picked that store to stake us out. I mean, he's trying to look all serious and everything, surrounded by fake hurl.

"I know what you mean," Page says as a skinny RediGard guy I don't recognize passes by. "The game's definitely over."

"They're waiting to ambush us," I say. "We'd get busted for sure if we tried anything now."

"It's too bad," Page adds in that philosophical tone she sometimes uses. "Freaking the customers out was kind of scary, but at the same time, I don't know, I got something out of it."

"Yeah, ten bucks a pop," I say.

"Nah," Marcus says. "I know what Page's talking

about. Standing up to people, letting them know that there are actually others out there who deserve respect and who'll take it—by any means necessary."

I know what Marcus and Page are saying, but for some reason it's too depressing to get into with them. All I know is that, bottom line, I'm out of work again. And, besides, quitting isn't necessarily the end of this . . . whatever it is we've been doing here. "There's just one problem," I say, and Marcus and Page sigh at the exact same time. I can hear a name in that anxious breath: Jimmy Biggins.

"Did he say for sure he wasn't going to stop?" Marcus says. "Because if he doesn't, and he gets caught . . ."

"I wouldn't worry about him ratting us out," I say. "It's not his style."

"And he's had a lot of practice being interrogated," Page adds.

No one says anything, and just sitting here with all the security guys swarming around us, especially Stu giving me the stink-eye from the Joker's Den, makes the stale air even stuffier, the floor wax more pungent, the Muzak more annoying. "Well," I say and stand, "I'm going to talk to the Chair, see if he'll spread the word that we're closing up shop."

"Good idea," Marcus says and gets up. He takes his time straightening the sleeves of his blazer, adjusting his glasses, tying one of his shoes—even though about a million RediGard eyes are watching him. I guess, like he said, he's used to it. "Anyone doing anything this weekend?" he asks as he and Page walk toward the south exit.

"No plans," I say. "Maybe I'll do some homework for

a change." I veer away from my friends and head for ShUSA.

⁓

About a hundred feet or so away from the store, I notice mall security chief Lance Hungerford standing right out in front, just a couple of steps from the carpeted interior. He rests his left hand on his hip and swings his radio in his right, as if ready to call in backup security at any second. He's facing in my direction. I don't know if he sees me or not, or if he's even looking for me, but why take chances? If Lance doesn't want me talking to the Chair tonight, I won't.

I cut across the mall, slalom through a few people, and loop back around in the direction I just came from, moving a little faster now. Stu has left the Joker's Den and is standing in front of the atrium fountain, tracking me as I pass. It's all I can do not to break into a sprint, but I don't want to alarm anyone. I wait until I've pushed through the exit doors before I start jogging.

Heading through the south lot, moving along the back of the building, I feel a bit lightheaded. Just being in the lot at this time of night, given the events of the past couple weeks, makes my stomach all jumpy. I keep my pace up, though, and replay in my mind the image of Lance standing in front of ShUSA, feet planted as if for a showdown. Was he, in fact, waiting for me? Or am I just being paranoid?

I'm startled by a man's voice barking obscenities in the night. The sound stops me dead.

Turning to look over the car roofs lined up at my right, I see someone in a Hello Kitty mask squared off with an

90

old man roughly his height. The old guy—in his late fifties, I estimate—struggles to get away, but Jimmy's got a firm hold on the guy's jacket. The old man's tweed cap slides back on his head.

I try to shout Jimmy's name, but the words don't form. Instead, I make a gurgling noise, which makes Jimmy look in my direction. Our eyes lock for a seemingly eternal second, and while Jimmy's turned away from the old man, the guy takes a swipe at the Hello Kitty mask, knocking it off Jimmy's face. Acting on reflex, Jimmy whirls around and punches the guy. The man drops like a textbook knocked out of some geek's hand in the hallway.

"Jimmy, no!" I shout, realizing a second later—a second too late—how stupid it was to shout his name. Bile rises in my stomach as Jimmy turns for the weeds separating the mall parking lot from the river and plunges down the embankment. The man on the ground moans and rolls in my direction, his eyes meeting mine. I bolt for the weeds.

The sound of the river engulfs me like jetwash, and I fight the urge to puke as I run alongside the raging water, not stopping until I reach the dark, rank-smelling tunnel underneath the Onion River Bridge. Jimmy's nowhere in sight. Where is he? Where did he go? Why did he have to hit that guy?

My heart pounds along with the car tires hitting potholes above me as I climb the embankment at the side of the bridge. I hide in the weeds just off the Winston-Riverside intersection, waiting for a break in traffic, each new set of tires running me over in my mind.

12

Weekends are supposed to help a person clear his mind, give him a break, some rest, all that stuff. But this past weekend might as well have never been on the calendar. Come Monday morning, I still have the same problems I had on Friday. Sure, I got some homework done on Saturday and Sunday—but not much, not with all this stuff about Jimmy on my mind. No one has seen him since he decked that guy at the mall. I called his house, but his mother hung up when I asked for him. I've sat on the Mound for hours. Nothing. He's basically disappeared.

Telling Marcus and Page about seeing Jimmy punch that guy didn't make the weekend any more pleasant. Now they're wigged that Jimmy'll get caught and rat us out. I don't think he'd do that, but I'd definitely feel responsible if he did.

That's why I spent practically all day Saturday just riding my bike around town, looking for him. It was weird, but just doing that, just cruising Shunpike Falls, brought back some nice memories of what life was like before the mall was built. Jimmy and I used to spend every weekend riding around, first down at Legion Park—the Mound seemed so much bigger then—and then up and down Winston Road.

The strip being what it is—a half-mile of fast-food franchises and gas stations, with a couple of cheap motels wedged in here and there—one night a week we'd spread whatever money we'd scraped together over a few different fast-food joints, making a banquet of the whole deal. I was getting a small allowance then, and Jimmy was pretty good at scrounging up returnable bottles and cans.

Anyway, we always got our burgers at McDonald's, especially once Jimmy figured out that if you ordered a burger without those lame-o little onions, they'd have to make it fresh instead of giving you one premade. At least that's what he'd heard. We'd cross Winston Road to get our shakes at Burger King, mainly because I decided they made them better there, though I can't remember now what made them any different from the McDonald's shakes. And for french fries, there was only one serious contender: Mo's Hots—then, and still, the only nonchain restaurant on all of Winston. Then we'd race back to the picnic table under the Legion Park rain shelter and eat. "Fast-food connoisseurs," my mother called us. If one of us had a little cash left over, we might get donuts at Dunkin' Donuts for dessert. Or maybe split one.

I guess Jimmy and I complained a lot back then about not having anything fun to do, but we seemed to have a pretty good time anyway. Still, we couldn't wait for the Onion River Mall to be built. No one could, except Mrs. Pegg, who regularly trashed the mall in her paper—and, of course, my father, who basically blew his real estate career on some stupid idea for a building project he claimed would be much better than a mall. Shunpike Common, he called it. The words haunt me to this day.

But today also presents its own unique challenges—or "ironies," as Framm might call them. Jimmy and I have gone our separate ways, and he mugged some old guy at the mall a few nights ago. At the same time, however, Marcus, Page, and I—until two weeks ago absolutely invisible on the school social radar—are now everyone's best friends.

As I walk down the hallway, kids I've never met say hello to me. One guy, a soccer player named Gary Pollino, gives me a wordless high-five as I pass him near the Senior Corner. I hear kids call out *"Caveat emptor!"* and "Mall Mafia—no fear!" as I bend over a drinking fountain or stand at my locker. Weird. Completely tweaked.

Turning away from my locker just now, I bump into Steve Uttley, an obnoxious and slightly dangerous kid who got kicked out of North Ridge Academy last year for torching the town gazebo. Rumor has it Uttley was the one who called in the bomb threats here at Shunpike High last month—the bomb threats that are probably going to cost us vacation days when the administration tacks them on at the end of the school year. Nice work, Uttley.

"Deeewwwd!" he says, punching me in the arm and bouncing back and forth on his feet, as if hippie dancing in those baggy jeans he always wears. "My mom is, like, *freaked* about this." He taps his fat head, which sports one of those stupid-looking mushroom-style haircuts.

"Your mom?" I say, closing my locker behind me. "Why?"

94

"*Deeewd*, she came home from the PTA meeting, like, convinced someone's going to blow up the mall."

"She did?"

"Well, you are, aren't you?" Steve opens his arms wide, as if to say, "Well, what are you waiting for?" He cackles that crazed laugh that never fails to make me nervous, no matter how far away from him I'm standing when I hear it.

"No. Actually . . . ," I start to say, but Steve's already on his way down the hall, cackling away and firing an imaginary gun at trash cans, water fountains, exit signs.

~

When I catch up with Page and Marcus in the cafeteria, the table is already cluttered with items obviously left there by kids who work at the mall—a bag of gummy bears, some jewelry, a couple of CDs. "Trick or treat," I say as I sit down.

Marcus slides a copy of the *Beacon* across the table. "Tell me," he says, "is this a trick or a treat?"

Most kids at school care as much about the *Beacon* as they do about the student handbook, which is not much, but looking around the cafeteria, I see copies of the newspaper strewn everywhere. I glance at the headline on the front page:

Airport Youth on Mall Rampage

Below, there's a picture of Jimmy that must've been taken in middle school, because he's giving the camera a "Say cheese" smile and he has short hair that looks like it was cut with a chainsaw. A tingle crawls along my neck as I read the photo caption: "James Biggins, 15, still at large and considered armed and dangerous."

"Armed? What the . . . ?" My hands begin to shake as I read on, noticing how Mrs. Pegg has expertly cast every single word to make the problem seem as serious as possible: mentioning that Jimmy lives in the Airport neighborhood, which everyone knows is where most of the trouble goes down; suggesting that he might be planning a larger attack on the mall—totally false. And this "rampage" he's supposedly on? The article makes it clear that Jimmy's responsible for *all* of the mall attacks, another complete lie—maybe even mathematically impossible. Pegg has made him into a monster, a mega-delinquent.

Reading further, I get to a paragraph about some unrelated trouble Jimmy has been in—minor things mostly, like stealing road signs, shoplifting, egging houses, and a brush fire he accidentally started while playing with matches behind Penny Pantry the summer we were ten. Someone's been keeping a pretty complete file on the kid.

The next paragraph has some quotes from the mall's executive director, Mr. Palmeroy, saying they suspected "this menacing intimidator" was responsible for "the recent unease," but that they hadn't wanted to "foster any unsubstantiated accusations by asking the police to intervene until now."

"What a joke," I say as a quote from Lance jumps off the page:

Said Director of Security Lance Hungerford:

"We've now turned the matter over to the police and Cedarbrook officials, and we're certain that with appropriate security measures in place, Biggins poses no further threat to mall patrons."

"Cedarbrook?" I say, the words coming out in a gasp.

Page gives me an icy scowl. "Yeah, how do you like that? The *Beacon* finally has some breaking news, but it means I'm going to juvie."

I can hardly breathe, let alone speak. If kids around here know nothing else, we know about the Cedarbrook School. And we know it has nothing to do with cedars, brooks, or school—and everything to do with straightening out some of the worst kids in the state: young murderers, rapists, arsonists, thieves. The "school" is a nasty place, so nasty I've never heard a single joke about it. My friends and I never talk about it, never walk through the woods west of the airport to look at it through the fence, which we could easily do, since it's not far from the end of the runway.

"Really, though, it's this last part that gets me," Marcus says. He points toward a spot almost at the end of the last column:

Biggins was questioned in connection with an assault on Valley Road earlier this month, which required the victim to be hospitalized. That attack is still under investigation.

I'm no journalist, but I can see Mrs. Pegg's strategy very clearly: She's giving readers one last thing to keep in mind whenever they hear the name Jimmy Biggins—Valley Road. "They can't do that. Can they?" I look at Page. "Link Jimmy to this other incident? Isn't that. . ."

"Libel?" Page folds the paper and gazes across the cafeteria. "If Mrs. Pegg published something she knew was false, that would technically be libel. But she didn't actually say Jimmy was guilty of the Valley Road assault. She merely implied it."

"Innuendo," Marcus says.

"But she said he was armed."

"Today, that's a reasonable suspicion about any kid old enough to hold a gun," Marcus adds. "How many guns do you think are in this building right now? In this *cafeteria* right now?"

"But she blamed him for all the mall . . ." I realize I'm starting to rant as other kids stare at me. I push the paper aside.

"Aha," Page says. "Now we're onto something. What's the incentive for blaming Jimmy for everything?"

"Public relations," Marcus answers in that smooth, confident lawyer's voice. "Think about it. Thanksgiving's not far away."

"So?" I say.

"So? So, the day after Thanksgiving is *the* most important shopping day of the year—the start of the Christmas shopping season. But if people think the mall is too dangerous . . ."

"But Palmeroy and Lance must know that Jimmy's not

98

solely to blame for this stuff," I say, trying to keep from ranting again.

"Oh, they know," Marcus says, tapping the newspaper with a fork. "Remember the way word traveled around the mall about what you were doing—"

"What *we* were doing."

Page shoots me a nervous look.

"Palmeroy and Lance?" Marcus nods at the newspaper. "Those guys definitely know."

"So why are they putting all the blame on Jimmy?"

"They're not," Page chimes in, sounding like she's following Marcus's train of thought just fine, which I am not. "You see, they mentioned Cedarbrook."

That tingle crawls around my neck again. "And?"

"It's a signal. A signal to you . . . and us. And if it works, it'll scare us from taking this thing any further."

"Then all they need to do is bring Jimmy down," Marcus says, "to make everybody in town feel like they've caught the bad guy. To make everybody feel like the good guys are doing their job."

I shake my head, my thoughts so tangled up I can't form words.

Marcus gives the newspaper another tap. "Do you think Jimmy's seen this?"

I shake my head. "He's not a real avid reader."

As soon as the words leave my mouth, some students begin chanting down at one end of the cafeteria: "Big-*gins,* Big-*gins,* Big-*gins* . . ."

"Martyr time," Marcus says with surprising calm, as if he's been expecting whatever is now happening. "Like

Malcolm X. Jimmy's sacrificed himself to the cause. He's a hero."

"Like Joan of Arc," Page says, a blaze in her eyes.

"Cause?" I start to feel dizzy. "What cause?"

Marcus looks toward the cafeteria door just as a mob of chanting students spills into the hallway and moves toward the lobby. "Whatever cause you've got."

As I stand up, the chanting sweeps over me like a wave: "Big-*gins,* Big-*gins,* Big-*gins* . . ."

13

The instant my last-period class, biology, is over, I bolt out of school and up to the mall. Lance's quote about getting Cedarbrook involved in this matter has me too freaked out to walk in through one of the normal entrances, so I sneak up to the ShUSA stockroom door and bang on it. After about a minute, the Chair lets me in. "Can't talk now," he says, hurrying up the aisle, grabbing a couple of boxes on the way. "But do not go away."

I climb my favorite ladder and wait.

About five minutes later, the Chair rounds the corner again, cursing under his breath. He stops midway down the aisle, pivots, and crams a shoebox into a gap in the wall, really putting his weight behind it.

"Let me guess," I say. "Your customer wants to check out a few other shops first."

He nods. "Customers plural," he says. "The Romeo and Juliet from hell." He puts his hands on his hips, striking a pissed-off pose. "'Honey, they're too shiny,'" he mimics. "'I think they're supposed to be shiny, Pumpkin.' 'Well, Sugar Plum, it's my wedding, and I don't want you wearing shiny shoes. Sir, can you make them any less shiny?' 'Not really, miss. These are patinas. They're *made* especially to look shiny. Many formal shoes, as you may have noticed, are designed to carry a bit of a . . . *sheeeen.*'" He stares at the wall of boxes in front of him and shakes his head. "And then she fixes me with this stare like I've just told her to expect flash floods on her wedding day. 'Come on, Cookie Pie,' she says and grabs her guy, there, by the arm. 'These people obviously do not appreciate the details that go into a wedding.' The guy says something like 'Snookums, I think they're just showing you what they've got here,' which is true, since I showed him every frigging formal shoe we carry, but she gets up in a huff, still giving me the stink-eye, and says, 'We'll go somewhere else, then, a store where they understand I am not some common customer who straggled in off the street. I am the *briiide.*'"

"Did you happen to see the *Beacon* today?" I say when the Chair finally pauses.

He nods. "Indeed. Suburban alarmism at its finest. You need to do something."

"Haven't I done enough? I mean, Jimmy's a fugitive, the adults think someone's planning to bomb the mall—"

The Chair gives my ladder a kick to shut me up. "Chill, Mitch." He pulls his calculator out of his jacket pocket and punches in a couple of numbers, counts under his breath. "You calm?"

"Yes."

"Okay. Here's the deal." He suddenly cocks his head toward the stockroom door.

I hear distant voices, as if a parade's coming down Riverside Drive. The Chair and I walk to the door. Little by little, the voices grow louder until they're forming those words that have been dogging me since lunch: "Big-*gins,* Big-*gins,* Big-*gins* . . ."

"That kid," the Chair says in a grave tone.

"Jimmy."

"Yeah." He walks to the door, opens it a crack, and peers out. "Get him here somehow."

"Get him here? I haven't seen him in almost a week."

I catch sight of people dashing by the open sliver of stockroom door—shoppers, teenagers, skateboarders—like images in a maniacal slideshow. Judging from the sound, thirty kids must be marching across the parking lot.

"Would you look at that," the Chair says, still peering out the door. "You didn't tell them to do this, did you?"

"No way."

"Well, it's happening, dude. And it looks like it's happening fast."

"What if I can't find Jimmy?"

The Chair pulls the door closed. "You will. He trusts you. You're the only friend he's got."

"Some friend," I grumble and approach the stockroom door. I lay my hands on it, as though checking a door inside a burning building. Hearing the chants mixing with explosive bursts of *"Caveat emptor!"* outside, I push the door open slightly again. I spot kids waiting to ambush unsuspecting shoppers, while others shout *"Caveat emptor!"* at people trying to seal themselves safely inside their cars. A band of ten or so students remain in a loose column, chanting "Big-*gins,* Big-*gins,* Big-*gins*" as they circle the parking lot like vultures.

"Head down to the river," the Chair says, giving me a

103

light shove out the door. "Don't talk to anyone about this, and stay out of sight."

The stockroom door slams behind me like a blast from a starting pistol. I run for the river like I've never run before.

"Plenty of Free Parking!"

14

A week later, another Monday afternoon, there's still no sign of Jimmy. I don't know if that's a good thing or a bad thing. I mean, on the one hand, he hasn't ratted out the Mall Mafia. On the other, he's my friend and I'd feel better if I knew where he was.

Jimmy's outlaw status has worked Shunpike High students into a frenzy. For the first few days after his picture appeared in the *Beacon,* school assemblies erupted in the "Big-*gins*" chant. Decker eventually canceled all assemblies "until further notice." He also banned Hello Kitty masks, which became an overnight fashion sensation. Hours o' Wonder sold out of them in one day. Decker's ban, of course, has had the opposite effect: not even a Hello Kitty tattoo would be considered as cool as one of those cheap plastic masks.

As I've roamed the school hallways like a lost dog, my mind completely empty of a plan, people have stopped me to ask about him, to see whether the police have caught him yet. I tell them two things:

First, the truth—that I don't know if he's been caught, although I called Cedarbrook once to see if he was on their roster of "students." He wasn't. I won't call again. I don't want to encourage them to start getting a cell ready for him.

Second, that I don't think people snapping on Hello Kitty masks and marching up Riverside Drive every day after school to terrorize shoppers is going to improve his situation.

When I'm lucky, people actually listen to the second part. But no one seems ready to stop just yet. Those kids differ in one crucial way from my friends and me: They don't get paid for harassing people. They do it for fun, or whatever. Evidently, it's the cool thing to do. Now that the cops have started cruising the parking lot, only the truly tweaked kids actually confront shoppers trying to get to their cars, and I'm told those incidents usually end with a police cruiser pulling up too late to catch those kids before they disappear down the riverbank. Everyone else just marches around, chanting "Big-*gins*, Big-*gins*," which, I guess, is legal. Basically, from the end of school every day—three o'clock—until the mall closes at nine, the place is under siege.

Mrs. Pegg published an article about those other kids in today's *Beacon*.

Mall in the Grip of Teen Terrorists

The smaller type beneath the headline said something like "Sales Sag As Assailant Eludes Authorities." Pegg rambled on about how none of this would've happened if the town had never built the mall in the first place, because what has it been, all along, but "a haven for idle minds lacking the will to do something constructive with their time." And what has it become but "an attractive target for Biggins' antisocial agenda." The same photo of Jimmy that ran with the first article appeared, a little smaller, midway down the column.

Page, Marcus, and I have agreed not to go near the mall, not until things cool down. Who knows when that will be? In the meantime, some mall salespeople have given me money to funnel to Jimmy when I see him—if I ever do. Sheila Burke has kicked in, along with Keith Sullivan, Louise Carruccio, and a few other salespeople. The cash goes right into the Jimmy Biggins Relief Fund in my pocket.

But where is he? On my way home from school, I check—for about the twentieth time—all the places he could be hiding: the park; the dump down next to the airport runway; the clearing in the woods that used to be a brickyard off Valley Road, where the burnouts have keg parties. Nothing. Walking along my street, I call out Jimmy's name, just in case he's watching from somewhere. It's making me crazy.

When I get home, I'm surprised to find both Mom and Dad sitting at the dining room table. They each have a mug of tea in front of them, but the way they look at me when I walk in the front door tells me they're obviously more interested in my coming home than in talking to each other. "Hey," I say, stepping into the uncomfortably quiet room.

"Hey, Mitch." Dad's voice croaks, as if he hasn't said anything in a while. His eyes shift suddenly to my Kourt Kingz, and I feel the blood rush to my face. "Nice sneakers," he says, then glances at Mom. "They look brand new."

Mom gives me a puzzled look.

"They are, sort of," I say. "They're red-tags. Factory defects. The price was drastically reduced."

"Oh," Dad says with a nod, then turns his attention to the paint stuck to the backs of his hands. "A shrewd purchase, then."

"Right." I find the biggest glass in the cupboard and pour myself some milk, taking my time drinking it down, bracing myself for a two-ton Parent Bomb.

"So, tell us," Mom says, "what's the poop on school?"

I swallow hard as a double twinge of embarrassment surges through my body: one for Mom's bizarre parental slang—poop?—and one for knowing that she will now, with Dad's support, bulldoze into my private life.

"School's fine," I say, but as I walk into the dining room doorway, my eyes meet Dad's, and I know I'm being given a chance to confess something before the interrogation begins. The question is, confess to what? How much do they know?

"Um, I'm doing all right," I continue. "Not great, but there are, you know, a couple of big projects coming up. So I've been laying the groundwork, you know, for those big projects."

"Mm. I see," Mom says.

"What about after school, Mitch?" Dad chimes in, giving their whole deal away, which is his specialty.

"After school?" I shrug. "You know, I hang out with my friends."

"You hang out," Dad repeats, rubbing his forehead with one paint-streaked hand. "Now, let me ask you this . . ."

Whether she realizes it or not, Mom gestures identically—the forehead in the hand. I'm tempted to do the same thing just to make it unanimous.

"Are you sure you're spending that time wisely?" Dad says, kneading his forehead as if it's a hunk of bread dough. "Are you sure all that time is in line with your . . . priorities?"

Maybe it's that word—*priorities*—or maybe it's just Dad's tone, but something in this exchange really tweaks me. I can tell from all the clues—Dad being all serious, head in his hand, Mom standing by his side, head in her hand—that I'm supposed to be reasonable and calm and apologetic for something. But tonight that's not what I'm feeling. I'm worried about my friend Jimmy, and whatever problem my parents have with that is just that—their problem.

I stay calm, though, hoping to keep this conversation as short as possible. "No," I say. "I guess my priorities are not in order. I could spend more time on my homework. That's my goal for this week."

"Oh, so you've got a goal for this week," Dad rants slightly and drums his knees. "That's great, because, I'll tell you what, I've got a goal for this week too—"

"Reg," Mom says, "please try to stay calm—"

"Oh, I'll stay calm," he interrupts, not that calmly at all. "I'll stay calm just as soon as someone explains to me just what in the hell is going on at the Onion River Mall."

He stares at me with wide eyes, so I turn to Mom and

110

give her my best "What's his problem?" look.

"I'm sure you've heard all about this awful business at the mall," she begins. "Some are calling it terrorism. Now, whether or not all of those stories are true—"

"Sally," Dad says. "I told you—"

"I know what you told me. But it's not unusual for people to exaggerate things a little at those PTA meetings. And that Rosemary Pegg with the *Beacon* doesn't always present the most balanced picture of things."

"What do you know about this, Mitch?" Dad says. "Now, we know *all* about your friend Jimmy Biggins, so don't even try to tell us you don't. But now, apparently, it's gone beyond that. There are dozens of these kids now in his little gang, and we're pretty sure that there's something bigger coming down the pike. These little terrorists have been warning customers about . . . something. They're not saying what they're warning everybody about. They're just saying, 'Let the buyer beware.'"

"Maybe they're just saying that, you know, to freak people out. Maybe they don't really plan to do anything else."

Dad just stares at me blankly for a few seconds, as if what I've just said doesn't compute in his brain.

"I mean, that's a possibility, right?"

Dad's stare lingers. "The mall," he finally grumbles, rising and pacing over to the living room window. He's obviously unimpressed with my theory. Sometimes his own theories just overwhelm him. This is obviously one of those times. "Worst thing ever happened to this town," he rambles to the dusky gray curtain falling over the street. "You've got all that bad air . . . and what about the

111

community businesses? Huh? Killed every local retailer from the river to the airport—overnight." He snaps his fingers. "Now all we've got is fast food out there on Winston. And sprawl. Five times the traffic this area was designed for. Tell me, did we fight the British for the luxury of spending all morning trying to make a left turn onto Winston Road? Did we?"

Go back to the firm, Dad. I focus my mental energies on him, like a guy I saw on a TV show who could bend metal objects with his mind. It's pathetic, I'll admit, but this is my last hope in communicating with my father—telekinesis. Admit you made a mistake, Dad. *The mall was the right plan, Dad. The community supported it, Dad.*

"And what kind of a community are we building there?" he babbles. "There were plans. Community plans. Develop the lot . . . and with Shunpike Common, a center, a real *downtown*—something this town's never had. Bring people *together*."

I try to scramble my thoughts in the white noise of an approaching jet. Times like this, it's impossible not to long for the days when Dad would come home in a shirt and tie and toss his briefcase on the sofa. There'd be backyard barbecues, a game of catch, all that stuff. Now he lives on another planet, not just in a trailer in another town.

"Reg," Mom says, "maybe tonight's not a good night for this."

"I've been saying that mall was trouble from the start," he hisses, turning to her.

"We know," Mom groans. "But, come on, it's not the mall's fault. It's what those kids are *doing* there—"

"Like that Jimmy Biggins," Dad fires back. "Oh, he's a real operator, that one. And anyway, Mitch and all these other kids could've had someplace to go without the mall." He turns back to the window. "They *could* have. Shunpike Common. We were working for that—"

"Honestly, Reg. Not tonight—"

"But people just wanted that mall—*man!*" Dad claps his hands so hard that I'm sure it stings a little. He glares accusingly at me. "Well, they're not liking it all that much right now. I can assure you of that."

I nod in agreement and wait for him to calm down, which takes awhile. When he's finally sitting again, I try one more time: "So, you don't think there's any possibility that nothing worse is going to happen at the mall, that this so-called warning isn't really a warning?"

"Oh, wake up, Mitch," Dad says. "Think. Would it really be so hard to plant a bomb in the mall, or maybe walk in there shooting—"

"A bomb?" I blurt out. "That's nuts—"

"Oh, is it now?" Dad says in that snide voice he sometimes uses when he's convinced he's right about something. "Is that really so far-fetched?" He fixes me with that annoying "Well, Mr. Smart Guy?" look. "You tell me, then, how many days of school you missed last year for bomb threats. Huh? How many? I want an answer—"

"Reg," Mom pleads, "I think you've made your point."

"I don't know," I say, realizing that he's got me in a pinch. Anything I say about the mall might tip him off to what I know. Right now, I don't trust myself to say anything about anything.

"Go on, Mitch," he needles. "Guess."

"Four—"

"Six. And you've missed three days already this year, and it's only October."

With Dad's eyes still fixed on me like lasers, I glance into the kitchen, where Mom's now busying herself with something—no doubt to avoid dealing with this situation.

Dad seizes the opportunity, like he often does, to share everything he *thinks* he knows: "They're saying there might be a connection with the Valley Road attack."

"They?"

"The police."

"Insane—"

"And I'll give you one guess who they're keeping close tabs on—"

"He didn't do it," I snarl, surprising myself with the sound. "Jimmy had nothing to do with Valley Road."

Dad narrows his eyes at me. "I thought you might say that." He glances into the kitchen and doesn't say anything else.

As if on his cue, Mom walks into the dining room and sets a plate of meat loaf and string beans on the table in front of me. "Eat," she says, "while it's still hot."

"Mitch . . . ," Dad adds in a softer tone as he begins picking at the paint on his hands, "your mother and I have been talking."

They've clearly rehearsed this conversation—these two people who otherwise can't get together to plan a trip to the grocery store. That fact, coupled with the obnoxious jet thunder passing over us, makes my heart start pounding.

114

"And?" I say.

"I hate to be a mean old hag, Mitch," Mom says as she tugs nervously at the tissue in her hands, which she's already pulled into a pile of shavings fit for a hamster cage. "But your father and I don't want you hanging around with Jimmy Biggins anymore."

The milk in my stomach churns as Dad stands and drifts back into the living room, where he stares out the window.

"Why?" I say, watching him for a response.

Mom brushes my hair back over my ear with her hand. "Because—"

"I asked why, Dad?" Blood lights up my body like a furnace. "Let me guess. He's a bad influence. Is that it?"

Dad doesn't turn, just keeps staring into the street. "Kid assaulted a man in the mall parking lot last week," he says grimly. "He's been terrorizing people at the mall for a month now."

I can't think of a response that won't get me in trouble. Air traffic crowds the void in my brain where I was hoping a good idea might form.

"I know this is bad news, honey," Mom says, "but we're just trying to help you make the right decisions."

The right decisions, I think and look at Dad. Even in the darkness, I can tell he's picking paint from his fingers. I can remember days when Mom and I would pick him up at the airport, when he returned from business meetings all over the region—in Boston, Albany, Toronto. All over.

"We just don't think he's a good influence," Mom adds, barely loud enough for me to hear her under the jet's roar.

I also remember Dad's partners at Shunpike Horizons,

a fairly successful real estate office. Even as a kid who knew nothing about anything, I knew those guys were jerks. I played with their sons and daughters in Legion Park, and those were some seriously spoiled brats.

"Influence," I practically spit across the room.

Dad looks at me for a second but doesn't say anything. As the jet screams by, he turns back to the street.

I take my plate to the kitchen, set it on the counter without taking a single bite, and leave.

15

From where I stand on the Onion River Bridge, the mall glows with sinister glamour: one part Las Vegas casino, one part nuclear power plant in the middle of a meltdown. The parking lot lights burn like stars against the blacktop and radiate into the sky, covering the mall in a hazy yellow dome. To give my mind something to think about besides the mess I've made of my best friend's life—and, quite possibly, the local economy—I wonder what the mall might look like to people on a riverboat, were one to come chugging down the Onion River out of the north.

Would the people see, off the port side, the bright glints in the glass of the pyramid-shaped atrium skylight, or the street lights beyond the mall, square-dancing two-by-two down the Winston Road strip to the airport? Would they think they were passing a bustling river city? A place you might actually want to visit?

The riverboat tourists might just as likely peer over the starboard side, to the south, and into the rolling hills of Queensbury, but what would there be to see? Old, dimly lit homes dotting shaggy meadows, the spire of the Queensbury College chapel poking from a cluster of stately roofs and widow's watches, ancient trees shaking their branches as if to say, "It's impolite to stare!"

Those passengers probably wouldn't realize that the mall bathed in this festive glow is about the lamest excuse for a mall ever built: a glorified warehouse, an L-shaped lump of dirty-white stucco that could've been designed by someone hoping to signal "Losers" to people flying overhead, warning them to stay away.

There, cutting in and out of the shadows of that mercantile mirage, is the chaos—"bedlam," in Pegg's words: customers running to their cars, skateboarders circling the lot, kids shouting in the night. War.

At least that's what it looks like from here, though part of it is probably just my paranoid imagination. Whatever is actually happening down there, I'm responsible for it. Yet, standing on the bridge as I have so many times before, I can't remember where I originally thought it might all lead. Maybe I forgot to think about that. Maybe that's the real problem.

I spit into the river. The river roars back, as if laughing.

What was that?

Something moving down by the riverside catches my eye. I scan the banks, watching to see if it happens again—

There.

Nothing: a dingy piece of plastic pasted up against a shopping cart.

Another breeze kicks up, and the sheet moves again. Just as I'm turning away, I see the hand holding it.

I run back across the bridge, into Shunpike Falls, and down the embankment. "Jimmy, it's me!"

"Mitch?"

"Stay there, dude. It's okay. I'm alone."

I scramble through the weeds to where he's huddled inside a lean-to made from two overturned shopping carts and a cardboard box, the plastic sheet working as a door flap. He's looked better. His face is streaked with dirt, almost as if he smeared it on for camouflage. His hair hangs in oily strips, and he's shaking.

"They said I was dangerous!" he hisses, his eyes bugging. "They're after me—"

"No one's going to get you." I take hold of his shoulders. "But we've got to find you a better hiding place."

He stares back in a daze, his breath reeking. "I didn't mean to punch that guy. It just . . . happened."

"It's okay," I say. "We can fix it. We're going to deal with this the right way." Whatever *that* means. "I'm going to find you someplace to stay—oh, wait. Here." Reaching into my pocket, I take out the Jimmy Biggins Relief Fund.

Jimmy stares at the money. "What's that?"

"It's for you. A bunch of people pitched in."

"Whoa," he says, taking the wad of cash and flipping through the bills.

"Yeah, there's, like, sixty bucks there."

"This is all for me?"

"Yeah. For food, whatever. No one knew where you were, man. You've become kind of a folk hero, like Paul Bunyan."

"But . . . why?"

"Why? I guess because you freaked out every parent in town, and, I don't know, kids are psyched about that? I guess. You're a rebel, an outlaw."

"Outlaw." He repeats the word, clenching the bills and

119

turning toward the mall. "I ain't ever going back there."

"Well, the Chair wants us to meet him in the stock—"

"No, I mean home. My folks. They can just go to hell."

"They probably will—"

"They beat me, Mitch." He turns toward the river.

"I know."

"No, I mean, they both beat me. Take turns. Pa'll hold me while Ma wails on me. That's why fricking Shane left."

I start to feel sick.

"They get good and drunk." Jimmy pulls his hair back with one hand and runs a finger along his scalp just above his hairline. "See this? Feel."

I reach up and run my finger along a ridge of flesh about as long and wide as a paper clip.

"Beer can. Nice, jaggedy, fricking crunched-down beer can, from about ten feet away."

"Your dad?"

He nods. "I was sitting there watching cartoons one Saturday morning, and *wham!*"

I just shake my head, not knowing how else to respond.

"Yeah. Pretty fricking serious."

He looks at me for a long time then, as if trying to decide if I'm really on his side. The way things are going, I can't blame him for being suspicious. Then, looking beyond me and up toward the mall again, he begins to cry. He actually begins to cry. Jimmy Biggins—crying. "I'm not dangerous," he chokes out.

I put an arm around him, don't ask me why. It just seems like the right thing to do. "You made a mistake, dude," I say. "People make mistakes. It's what we do."

～

I can hear the Chair's key turning in the lock of the stockroom door just as I start pounding on the other side.

"Wha!" he shouts, scuffling back a few steps. I hear his
keys fall onto the floor. "What are you trying to do, give
me a heart attack?" A couple of seconds later he says,
"Who is it?"

"Mitch."

The key turns in the lock again.

"We're closed," he says as he peers out a sliver of door.
"And you should *definitely* not be here. This place is very
hot right now—"

"I've got Jimmy." I push past him and into the stockroom.

"For real?"

"Yeah, he's been living like a slug under some plastic,
over near the bridge."

"Is he okay?"

"He'll be a lot better when he's got a better hiding place,
somewhere the raccoons won't get him. So, what's the
plan?"

The Chair doesn't say anything right away, doesn't even
jingle his keys. The only sound is the flickering fluorescent
light overhead, the one with the bulb about to go dead.
The Chair stares at the light, turning slightly so he's looking at the bulbs from a different angle, as if he hasn't studied them light from every possible angle in the month or
so he's been obsessed with it.

"I'm responsible for him," I finally say, letting the
agitation creep into my tone. "I'm desperate."

"Desperate." The word snaps the Chair out of his

121

fluorescent-light zone. "Right. Bring him up here."

"And then what?"

"He'll stay at my place for a while, till things cool down."

"You'll do that?"

Again, the Chair is silent as he paces up the aisle and back again, examining the shelves as if taking inventory. Then he turns and stares at the stockroom door. "You say he's close by?"

"Yeah, down by the river."

"Can you get him up here in five minutes?"

"Less. I'll go get him right now." I walk to the door and peer outside, making sure the coast is clear. Just before I bolt for the embankment, I glance back at the Chair.

He's pacing the aisle again, calm as can be, even though I'm about to deliver Shunpike Falls's Most Wanted right to his doorstep.

I can't say for sure, but there's something definitely tweaked about this whole situation.

As I sprint back across the parking lot, I try to remember what it was like when this place was nothing more than a shopping mall. It was never a very good mall, but still . . .

～

I'm relieved to find Jimmy still waiting on the edge of the weeds, just beyond the glow of the parking lot lights. "It's all set," I say. "He's going to take you to his place until things cool down."

Jimmy stares across the lot toward the stockroom door, where the Chair now stands with his back to us, fumbling with his keys. "I don't like that guy," he grumbles. "I don't trust him."

"You don't have to like him," I say. "And we don't have any choice but to trust him."

The Chair turns and walks toward a beat-up black Audi about fifty yards away. It's one of twenty or so cars still scattered throughout the lot. He glances around, making sure the coast is clear.

"Should I make a break for it?" Jimmy says, stepping into the light.

The Chair sees him. I yank him back into the weeds. "He'll swing by," I say. "Man, you've got to get used to staying hidden."

The Audi's engine fires up, making a rasping, high-pitched screech as the Chair guns it a couple of times. I have to admit, it's not exactly the sound one associates with the term "high-performance automobile."

"Nice ride," Jimmy says with a sarcastic snort.

The Chair leaves his headlights off as he angles the car in our direction.

"Deal with it," I mutter back as the Audi slows down, approaching us along the edge of the lot. "You're not exactly going to the prom."

"All Sales Are Final"

16

"Perhaps Mr. Grant has the answer . . ." The voice floats like a mosquito around my head as I sit in history class Monday morning, staring out the window and onto the soccer field. "Mr. Bad Gas" is riding me, but I still can't pull myself away from the idea of the cops cruising the streets of Shunpike Falls looking for Jimmy. I mean, the kid really is *wanted.* Everywhere I go, I hear adults talking about him—the teachers here especially.

Jimmy's got a good hiding place, but what does he do all day? Isn't he imprisoned, in a way, at the Chair's apartment, wherever that is? And who knows, the Chair's crib could be a real dump.

I've got to say, though, that our classmates aren't helping this thing cool off. Every day after school, they march right back up there to the mall parking lot and hang around, verbally abusing customers, chanting Jimmy's name. Great. Like so many trends that have swept through school, the events at the Onion River Mall are now following their own mysterious course. When will it end? *Will* it end?

"Mr. Grant?"

Muffled laughter.

"Mr. Grant." A hand on my shoulder directs me away from the window.

More muffled laughter.

My eyes travel up Bad Gas's gorilla-hairy, tattooed arm to the frowning ex-Marine at the end of it. "You'd rather not participate today? Is that it?"

"I'm sorry, Mr. LaGasse. I'm just really tired."

"Tired." He looks deep into my eyes while my classmates giggle to themselves. Some emotion seems to register in the hard features of his face as his nostrils twitch. "Yes, your eyes do look a little red," he says, loud enough for the rest of the class to hear, as if this is supposed to freak me out. He obviously thinks I'm baked. "Perhaps you'd like to go down to the health office, then. Have them give you the once-over. I'll call Ms. Heath right now." He smiles coolly.

"Yeah, I think that's a good idea," I say.

His smile droops. He frowns again, hostile, challenged.

I stand up and stretch. "I don't know what it is, but I just can't wake up. Health office. Definitely."

~

I pass Ms. Heath's twenty-questions interrogation easily, convincing her that I'm not stoned, just anxious, stressed out, and sleep-deprived. So she hands me a brochure on the importance of a healthy breakfast and lets me spend the rest of the period in the health office. I lie back as comfortably as possible on the starchy bed sheets and think about Jimmy. It actually starts to make me a little sick to my stomach—the idea that the whole town hates his

127

guts, all because of my stupid idea to make a few bucks. The town has never loved him, it's true, and I did try to convince him to stop when things heated up at the mall, but, still, if it weren't for me and that Ginger and my big, smart mouth, none of this would've happened.

About the only thing that keeps me from losing my mind completely is the slim chance that I might be able to figure out a solution to this problem. A solution that stops the chaos at the mall, gets Jimmy off the hook for the whole thing, and keeps him, me, Page, and Marcus out of Cedarbrook. Right. *When pigs fly.* As my dad likes to say.

Fortunately, my break in the health office is followed by my lunch period, so I have a little more time to think before my next class. When I reach the cafeteria, it dawns on me that in my obsession about Jimmy and the mall, I forgot that the *Beacon* comes out today. Sure enough, copies are already strewn about the lunchroom. I find Marcus and Page at our usual table.

"Hey, Mitch," Marcus says. "Big news." He folds a paper open in the middle and slides it toward me.

Scanning the columns of a long article about a new leash law for pets, I don't see what Marcus is talking about at first.

Reaching across the table, he points to a small advertisement, about as big as a baseball card, in the lower-left-hand corner of the page. The headline reads,

Concerned Citizens:
Let's Stop the Mall Mayhem—Together!

The words running beneath it read,

A local group is forming to discuss ways to end the current crisis at the Onion River Mall. As community members, we have a responsibility to act. Are you interested in being part of the solution? A peaceful solution? A solution that restores civility to Shunpike Falls? We can do it only if we work together! Contact me to indicate your interest and availability.

Sincerely,

Reginald Grant
Rocky Town Acres, #22
Quarry
861-2066

In the lower-right-hand corner of the ad there's a blurry, dark picture of my father. My face lights up like a Bunsen burner. "What was it you said the other day, Marcus? 'What this country needs is more free speech worth listening to'?"

"I was quoting Hansell B. Duckett. But don't be so quick to judge, Mitch. This may be a good thing in the long run. At least he's out there trying to make things right. And everyone knows how much he hates the mall."

"I think it's very big of him," Page says. "He does it because he cares—"

"Why?" I snap. "Why does he care? No one cares about

him! That's just pathetic. That's just asking to be kicked."

Page rests a hand on my shoulder. "Try not to be so critical. Like Marcus says, he's trying—trying to bring people together. A lot of men don't even try. A lot of *women* don't."

I lay my head down on my arms and just breathe. The darkness is inviting, tempting me to pretend this is all a bad dream, that one of my best friends isn't hiding like some scared dog, that my father isn't doing his best to destroy an already ruined reputation, and that I have nothing to do with bringing my hometown to the brink of economic collapse. It's a lot to have on my shoulders. Too much. And that doesn't even take into account my missing history homework.

"I need someone to do me a favor," I say, even before I'm conscious of a coherent thought in my head.

"Mitch," Marcus says in a cautious tone. "What are you thinking?"

"I need someone to make a phone call for me."

17

There seems to be one parcel of land in every town that's cursed for business. "Chapter Eleven Corner," my father calls these places, since Chapter Eleven has something to do with bankruptcy. In Shunpike Falls, Chapter Eleven Corner is a one-story, flat-roofed, cinder-block building about three quarters of a mile out the Winston Road Extension, just beyond the bus line. Mrs. Pegg occasionally writes articles about that parcel, mainly because strip clubs sometimes try to open there, which she's against, of course. Dad once told me she ends up doing those club owners a favor by giving them free publicity, since people otherwise might not know anything's going on there, stuck out on the Extension the way it is.

Still, as far as I can remember, no business has survived at that location for more than six months or so, although Ye Olde Yankee Gun Shoppe hung on a bit longer, maybe because the building looks like the perfect place to store arms and ammunition.

The newest venture to gamble on that piece of real estate is the Shunpike Falls "Texas" Steak House, which opened a couple of months ago. As I walk the Extension in the fading afternoon light, I'm relieved to see beer signs glowing in the windows. At least the place is still in business. Business is hardly booming, though. Only three vehicles dot the slick new blacktop. One of them is Dad's truck.

Inside, the steak house is more like a smokehouse, with a mattress-thick layer of cigarette smoke crawling along the ceiling out of the bar off the entranceway. I peer into the bar but don't see Dad, just a couple of guys drinking beer and watching football on TV. The restaurant's on the other side of a chest-high swinging door, like the kind on a horse stall. I grab a copy of the *Beacon* from on top of one of those cheesy Love-o-Meter machines in the foyer— you know, you put a quarter in a slot and a light bulb flashes next to "Hot Stuff," "Cold Fish," or whatnot. I can see Dad over the top of the horse door, so I push on through.

Dad's one of four other people in the dining room. He spots me right away, and as I weave around the tables toward his booth in the back, he squints through the haze. "Mitch?"

"Hey."

"Fancy meeting you here. Wait, let me guess. You're looking for a dish-washing job or something, a little under-the-table stuff. Well, there's no harm in that, I suppose."

Before I can respond, he's smiling, shaking his head, and swirling ice cubes in his glass. "You know, most kids today expect things to be handed to them on a silver platter—"

"Dad—"

"But it doesn't work that way, does it, bub? No, sir. Never has."

I sense a lecture coming on. Ordinarily, this would be a good time to change the subject, but I know I can't. Besides, Dad notices the *Beacon* in my hands and tugs it from my grasp.

"Did you see my ad, Mitch?"

"Yeah, I saw it—"

"I had to do something. You know? I mean, someone has to do something. The quality of life in this town just keeps slipping and sliding."

"Right."

"And I'm willing to do *my* part to help out."

"I know—"

"I mean, Thanksgiving's only, what, less than three weeks away?"

"Something like that."

"You know what that means, don't you?"

"Yes—"

"Now, part of me really wants to tell someone 'I told you so' about that mall, but I'm looking at the big picture now. I can put my personal complaints aside for the sake of the community. Tell you what, though, it's awfully hard to build community without economic vitality. And, trust me, if those stores at the mall aren't crammed full of customers on the day after Thanksgiving, it's going to be a long, cold winter for everybody around here. There isn't going to be much neighborliness to go around—"

"Dad." I take the newspaper out of his hand and lay it on the table. "I'm here about your ad."

"What . . ." He gives me a puzzled look, cocks his head to one side. "What do you mean?"

"A girl I know called you for me, you know, to set this meeting up. I'd have called you myself, but I thought you'd freak. So, here I am."

Dad seems to become amused, then confused, then furious all in roughly five seconds. He shifts his attention to the ad, then back to me, then back to the ad, then back to me again, finally narrowing his eyes like I haven't seen since the day he found out his old business partners were suing him. "Help me out here, Mitch," he says in a rough voice. "Now, she said she had some connection to these . . . Are you telling me that you're . . . one of them? Is that what I'm hearing?"

I stare deep into his eyes, reaching way back for the reasonable man I don't see that often anymore—the one who used to come home, day after day, with a smile for his kid and time for a game of catch in the yard: the man who could listen and understand. "It's not as bad as it seems," I say. "Well, it's pretty bad. But it didn't start out that way."

Shaking his head, Dad takes a napkin off the table—they're cowboy bandannas—and begins wrapping it around his hand. "Why?" he says, his tone a little softer now.

As I search for some way to explain this mess, I watch the smoke roll like fog into the restaurant. A waitress approaches our table, but I shoo her off. She gives me a cross look, then loops back toward the swinging stall door. *Yeah,* I think, *you wouldn't expect a family with*

134

only one kid to have a black sheep. But we do—and I'm it.

"Those kids at the mall . . . ," I start to say.

"The terrorists." Dad's eyes widen. "*You* terrorists."

"No, not them—I mean, not us. I'm talking about the *other* kids at the mall."

Dad groans and looks at the ceiling. "You mean to tell me there are *other* kids?"

"There are kids who actually work at the mall, as in *real* work."

Dad squints across the restaurant for a second, then turns back to me. "What do you mean, 'real work'?"

I take a deep breath. "Uh, well, the salespeople were approached by those . . . uh . . . some kids who volunteered . . ."

Dad shakes his head again. "Why? Mitch, why would you volunteer to do that?"

I pick up a bandanna and wrap it around my hand. "Well, maybe *volunteer* isn't the right word."

His eyes widen again. "They *paid* you to harass the shoppers?"

I nod. "A few of us. The first . . . few of us. And, well, I was the very first."

Dad winces as if I've just plugged him with a six-shooter underneath the table. "That's . . . you're like . . . a hit man."

I turn away. "We didn't do it for no reason, you know. You should see the way some people treat those kids who work at the mall—just because they can, just because those kids are supposedly there to *serve* them."

135

"Hmm. So this was a kind of payback."

I nod and look at him. His expression has relaxed a bit, as if some of what I'm saying actually makes enough sense for him to follow. "Anyway, we tried to end it weeks ago. But, you know, when Jimmy crossed paths with that guy in the parking lot—"

"That boy's in a world of trouble."

"He's sorry."

"I don't think that matters a whole lot to the man over on Valley—"

"Jimmy didn't have anything to do with that. He told me so himself."

"Well, what do you think he's going to tell you, that he *did* do it?"

I feel the blood rush to my face as that know-it-all tone creeps into Dad's voice. "Listen," I say, trying very hard not to rant, "either you say you believe me about Valley Road, or this conversation's over."

Dad stares at me for a long time, obviously weighing his options. Eventually he nods. "I believe you, son. But—"

"No buts—"

"To the people looking for him, Jimmy's as good as guilty for Valley Road."

"I know," I grumble, "and that's totally unfair. The only thing Jimmy's guilty of is being worse off than the rest of us."

"How so?"

"He didn't want to stop bugging people at the mall when we did. The kid needs the money pretty much to survive, since he spends so much time out of the house."

"How much money?"

"Ten bucks a pop."

As Dad winces again, I regret my choice of words. He turns toward the horse-stall door and says nothing.

I don't know what to say either, so I gaze toward the cafeteria-tray-size window in the cinder wall nearest us. I can't imagine much light shines through that grubby little hole. I don't see any answers flooding in here either.

"I'm sorry," Dad says in a slightly unsteady voice as he turns back to the table and works that bandanna around his hand some more. "I wish I had more to give you these days, but things are just really tight. The damn firm cleaned me right out. And I know your mother's in the same boat."

"I know."

"I'm trying to get it together. You realize that, don't you?"

I nod, looking away again.

"But people around here, they don't cut a guy many breaks."

"They're ruining Jimmy Biggins' life." When I turn back to Dad, he gives me a look I remember from a long, long time ago: the one that suggests he might actually understand me. Might.

"Yeah," he says, "that's something they're capable of. People didn't used to be like that." He clenches his bandanna hand like a boxer getting ready to don the gloves. "I guess that's why I'm here."

Here. The way he says the word suggests many different meanings: *here* at this restaurant, *here* in his pathetic financial circumstances, but also *here* in his role as the laughing stock of Shunpike Falls—all for wanting *here* in this town to mean something better than it does.

"I made a mistake," I say. "Can you help me fix it?"

He unclenches his fist and lets the bandanna fall to the table. "Sure. That's easy."

"It is?"

"Absolutely." He chomps ice cubes for a few seconds, then slides out of the booth. "Come on. Let's get this sorted out."

Needless to say, I'm skeptical. I mean, the man who "wishes he had more to give me" isn't the least bit fazed by the challenge to "get this sorted out"? What does he know that I don't? Are we talking about the same catastrophe? Whatever the case, I have no choice but to give him a chance. That's how desperate I am.

I follow him out of the restaurant.

∼

As we stand in the parking lot by Dad's truck, both of us silent, I look down Winston Road toward the tangle of fast-food restaurants on the horizon. From a distance they resemble a child's colored-pencil scribbles on the fading, gray backdrop of our town—some angry little kid messing up a wall out of sheer spite.

"Here's the deal," Dad finally says in a tone that strikes me as sincere in a way I haven't heard that often lately—not a lecture, not a scolding, just take-it-or-leave-it advice. "I'm going to help you." He gives me a sad look, as if he's already concluded that he's about to let me down. "I'm going to take you to the police."

I stare at him for a few seconds, and when I start to

object, he cuts me off: "It's the only way, Mitch."

"The only way to what, Cedarbrook?"

"You don't know that they'll send you there."

"But you don't know that they won't."

At this, Dad watches a jet's blinking light cut across the sooty early-evening sky. He doesn't say anything for the longest time, and I know he's struggling with something deep inside, which is the only time he ever shuts up. "But even if they do," he says in that rough, unsteady voice again, "that wouldn't be the worst thing."

"Easy for you to say."

He turns to me. "No, it's not."

I look down at the ground.

"You're all I've got, Mitch."

I keep staring at my Kingz, one of which is already coming unstitched around the toe.

"But, you know what? On second thought, you're right." A sudden lift in his voice makes me look up at him. "It is easy for me to say, but not for any reason you know about." He gazes down Winston Road again. "You need to get home right away?"

"No. Mom's covering for someone on the next shift."

Dad jingles the keys in his pocket—a habit I've actually missed a little. "Let's take a ride, then."

"Where are we—"

"Never mind just now. Hop in the truck."

He seems in a hurry all of a sudden, and it worries me.

～

We drive in silence to a cow pasture right on the Shunpike Falls town line, a scrap of land I've passed a million times on my way out to Dad's mobile home but never paid

139

much attention to. "Come on," is all he says as he pulls onto the shoulder and gets out.

I follow him across a ditch, under a rusted electric fence, and into the middle of a field. Seeming focused on a dark cluster at the summit, he leads me at a slight angle cutting across and up a small hill. "Almost there," he says every few steps through the damp, thick weeds.

As we near the cluster of dark shapes, I detect the vague outline of a tiny house about the size of the place where Mom and I live. At first, it looks like the building has fallen over on its side, but as I step into what must've been a yard, I can tell the house that once stood here burned down. I enter through a charred doorway. Dad follows me and walks into a corner of the space, where he leans against a low wall.

"I guess you've been out here before," I say.

"Oh, yes," Dad says with a heavy sigh.

While I explore a little, kicking boards aside to the sound of nails rolling on the floor and glass crunching underfoot, Dad stands in the corner facing the field and the road.

"I won't say, 'When I was your age . . . ,'" he begins in a low, gravelly voice, "because I wasn't your age." He crunches a few steps closer to me. "I was a little older. Just a little. But still old enough to know better. This was before I met your mother. I was still kind of crazy—or maybe bored is more like it. Anyway, a few buddies and I came out here one night."

He gestures with a sweep of his hand over the land we've just crossed. "This used to be a working farm—not

140

a very big operation, but, anyway, this building was the hired man's place."

"What were you doing out here?"

Dad turns to me. "We came out here to . . . tip cows." He shakes his head. "Whatever that meant. We'd heard about it, but none of us had ever done it. At any rate, we came up to our first cow, thinking that she'd be asleep. That was how the trick went: When a cow falls asleep standing up, with her knees locked, you can push her right over with a good shove. Problem was, this cow wasn't asleep. She turned her big head in our direction as soon as we laid hands on her. Scared us nearly half to death."

In my mind, I hear Page laugh: *Serves you right.*

"What'd you do?" I say.

Dad lets out another heavy sigh. "Well, after we picked ourselves up from laughing, we didn't know what to do. I mean, we just felt so stupid standing there, this cow looking at us as if she knew exactly what we were up to." He jams his hands in his pockets and kicks a nail across the floor. "If only we'd left it at that."

He leans back and looks into the sky. "So, this buddy of mine—not a bad guy, necessarily, just a bit wild—he lights a cigarette. Well, when the match caught, the cow spooked, took a few steps to one side. We thought that was about the funniest thing we'd ever seen. I can't explain why. We were young and stupid. Anyway, pretty soon this same guy gets the bright idea to snap one of those matches at the old heifer, you know, to see how fast she could move. Frankly, we were surprised at how quickly she'd started at the sight of the match flaring up."

Dad pauses, and in that moment I imagine the grass and weeds outside this little hovel catching fire.

"What happened then?"

"It's a miracle no one was hurt," Dad says, "but a good part of this field burned and . . . "

"This house." Acid churns in my stomach.

"Yes," Dad says. "An old farmhand. Poor old guy."

"Was he . . . "

"He wasn't hurt, no. I can't imagine it was any good for him, though, all that racing around trying to save his . . . his place here."

"Did you help him?"

"No. No, son. I didn't help him." Dad walks out through the remains of the doorway. "I was afraid," he says. "I didn't know what to do. And besides, my buddies piled back in our car. If I'd stayed around, they'd have stranded me."

Some friends, I think, exiting the ruined building.

"But that's not even the worst of it," Dad goes on. "The worst part was, I never told anyone what I'd done. Not until it was too late."

"Did you get caught?"

"No. But that almost didn't make any difference. At least not to me, it didn't. I tried to forget about it, tried to convince myself that it would all just disappear from my memory one day." Dad laughs bitterly to himself. "I don't know what I was thinking. You'd have to be an idiot to think you could get away with something like what we did. I mean, is there a kid *alive* who can keep a secret like that?" Dad looks back toward the shack. "I'd have been caught sooner or later. But, lucky for me, I guess, I decided to 'fess up. The whole thing was just eating me up inside."

"You turned yourself in?"

"Yup. Not for any other reason than I wanted to tell that poor old farmer I was sorry."

"And how'd that go?"

Dad turns to me again, his face a black mask of shadow. "It didn't go, Mitch. When I went to the police, I asked what'd happened to the guy, if I could make restitution."

"What's restitution?"

Dad stares at his feet, hidden in weeds, for a couple of seconds. "Repair. Repair the damage I'd caused. But the police said the old guy had moved on. No one knew where."

Neither of us says anything for what seems like an hour. I sort of automatically drift away from my father, imagining more vividly with each step the scene he's just described. In my mind, the old farmer resembles our head custodian at school, Mr. Girabaldi: He runs in no particular direction—rather, in all directions at once—shooing his cows to safety, scrambling around the periphery of the burning field, stopping to stare across the blaze to where I stand now, staring back at him.

I glance toward the road, imagining Dad running away, laughing his head off.

When I turn back to the farmer, his body melts in the flames.

A breeze kicks up, riffling burned papers in the wreck behind us. It seems like a signal to leave, so we start down the slope and across the field.

After we've slipped under the rusty fence and crossed the ditch, Dad turns back to the house again. "I paid a fine and did some community service," he says. "But I'll tell you, the worst punishment in the world couldn't match not being able to tell that man I was sorry. I mean, I don't even *know* what harm I did him." He leans on the truck and looks at me for a long time. "Things could get worse, Mitch. Someone could do something really stupid, and it'd be partly your fault. I say, nip this mall problem in the bud. Turn yourself in."

Dad climbs into the truck, but I linger by the roadside. I look toward the horizon, bugged by something he said back at the burned shack—something about being afraid of getting left behind to take the blame.

"You okay, Mitch?" he says, his hand resting on the key as he waits to turn the ignition.

"Yeah," I say. "Just thinking."

"I can understand." He starts the truck and stares ahead, as if looking back in time. "It's a big decision, so go ahead and sleep on it," he says. "But realize that if you don't stop this trouble while you still can, you may be sleeping on it for the rest of your life."

I don't say anything as we drive away. My mind is already made up. Tipped-over cows and burned grass don't have much to do with me, but I definitely know what I've done wrong. And I know who deserves an apology for being left behind. It's not an old farmer, it's not a rude mall shopper, and it's not the cops. If fact, it's nobody older than fifteen.

18

"So, let me get this straight," Marcus says, pacing back and forth at the foot of the Mound. "You think we should confess to what we did over there?" He stops abruptly, points across Legion Park in the general direction of the mall, and fixes me with a stern look in the dull glow of the lights reaching us from the basketball court. I swear, if he were just a little taller, you'd think he was a lawyer, not just a teenager who's definitely going to become a lawyer.

"My father's taking me down to the station after school tomorrow," I say, "if that's what I finally decide."

"But you haven't finally decided?" Marcus says in that superior tone that I don't really care for.

"I've decided," I say. "I was just hoping that we could all go in together, Jimmy included."

"And that actually makes some sense to you, Page?" Marcus rants, turning to where Page sits a few feet further up the Mound.

She shrugs, her head resting on her arms. "He makes a good point, Marcus. I mean, do we actually think we're going to get away with this forever?"

"But don't you see," he says, "we're not solely responsible anymore. There's a lot of blame to go around. Every day, the odds get better that if someone gets caught, it's going to be someone other than us—"

"It's going to be Jimmy," I interrupt. "Justify this to yourself any way you like, but if anyone's going to take the fall, it's Jimmy, and that's not fair. We can't bail on him."

Marcus and I lock eyes for a second. "Why postpone the inevitable?" he says, turning away. "Kid's going to end up in jail sooner or later."

I spring to my feet, but Page manages to grab the tail of my sweatshirt before I get very far. Marcus whirls around and takes a few quick steps back, his eyes widening as if he's just seen a ghost. A lunatic is more like it.

"Who the hell do you think you are?" I shout, the words flying out of my mouth by their own power as I drag Page a couple of feet toward Marcus.

"Take it easy," she says, finally getting a firm enough grip to stop me.

Marcus and I stare at each other for a while, with no one saying anything. A jet screeches faintly on the horizon, growing louder second by second, as if some cruel deejay in the sky is slowly bringing up the volume.

"Damn, Mitch," Marcus finally says. "I didn't mean anything by it."

"You did mean something by it." I grab a rock off the ground and fling it down into the playground, where it rings off the swing set. "You've written Jimmy off, just like everyone else around here." I face Marcus again.

He's staring at the ground.

I look at Page, and she's staring at her shoes.

"I'm going to the mall," I say, glancing at my watch.

"As soon as the Chair closes up, I'm having him take me to get Jimmy. I'll bring him back here. If you're with us, fine. If you're not, fine. But just so you know, I'll need all the help I can get convincing him to end this insanity." I start heading for the cut-through behind Pizza Hut.

"Mitch," Marcus says, his voice rising to compete with the approaching jet thunder, "what could we possibly tell the police that won't get us all sent off to Cedarbrook?"

"I'm sure you'll think of something," I shout back. "You always have something smart to say!"

～

I might just be paranoid, but I swear there are more police cruisers on the streets tonight. I know, from hearing teachers in the hall talking about Jimmy, that adults around town are really tweaked about him still being on the loose. I can just imagine what Mrs. Pegg is getting ready to publish about Jimmy in next week's *Beacon*—

Airport Teen Leads Martian Attack

Slinking around behind Pizza Hut, I cut through my secret passage of fast-food-joint back lots, out of view from the street. When I get to the corner of Winston and Riverside, I'm just a hundred yards from the mall—a straight shot across Winston, then down the embankment to the Onion River Bridge piling. From there I can approach the mall through the weeds lining the river.

I wait for the lights to change, look both ways for cop cars, and make a break for it.

I sneak along the weeds, peering into the eerie calm of the mall parking lot. Closing time. Even the lights in the

147

lot seem to glow more dimly, as if running on emergency power. I hope I'm not too late to catch the Chair.

Just as I'm about to bang on the stockroom door, a police cruiser pulls into the lot, so I sprint down into the weeds again, just to be safe.

I resurface after the cruiser has circled the mall once and then pulled back onto Riverside. I pound on the stockroom door a few more times, and the Chair opens it a crack. He seems more annoyed than startled to see me. Behind him, I'm surprised to find Jimmy up on a ladder, one arm stacked with shoeboxes, the other hand slotting them into the shelves.

"I see you've got a new employee," I say, pushing past the Chair.

"Everyone sleeps much better after an honest day's work," he says. "You're not supposed to be here."

"What's up, Jimmy?"

Jimmy just flips his chin at me and keeps working.

"Are you paying him under the table?" I say to the Chair, who's already found a stack of papers to inspect instead of actually listening to me.

"Who are you, the IRS?" he says. "This is a business, not a charity. Jimmy has been staying at my place—a place I pay rent on. Get it?"

"Yeah, I get it. You thought you'd pick up some free slave labor."

"In life, Mitch, you get what you negotiate for."

Spotting a column of boxes on the floor, I pick them up and hand them to Jimmy. "Well, we're about to enter into some negotiations of our own," I say. "Jimmy, I'm sorry I left you on your own. You can stay at my house tonight."

148

The Chair gives me a lightning-quick glance over his spreadsheets, but I totally catch him.

"By this time tomorrow," I add, leaning against the wall of shoeboxes midway between the Chair and Jimmy, "this'll all be over."

The Chair does something truly unusual: He stuffs his spreadsheets into the shoebox wall and gives me his undivided attention. "Is that right?" he says.

I glance at the flickering fluorescent light. "Yeah," I say and take a deep breath. "We're going to the police station."

Jimmy halts halfway down the ladder.

"You've decided you'd like to finish your high school career at Cedarbrook?" the Chair says.

I give Jimmy the most reassuring look I can. "We don't know what the punishment will be. But whatever it is, we're ready for it."

"Who's we?" the Chair says. "You mean that brainy black kid and the chick—"

"And Jimmy too," I say. "All of us. We're going in. Tomorrow after school. We're pulling the plug—"

"Digging your grave's more like it," the Chair says. "You think the cops are going to be lenient because you're confessing? What would you tell them anyway? That you've learned your lesson?"

I can feel the blood rising to my face with each stinging, slapping word from the Chair.

"Well, here's what I know about a lesson," he sneers. "A lesson is what you get when you don't get what you want."

Jimmy stops climbing just one rung from the floor, as if

149

he'll go scooting back up the ladder if my debate with the Chair takes a turn he doesn't like.

"Or have you guys not noticed," the Chair says, walking slowly toward me, "that there are cops patrolling the mall, looking for one Jimmy Biggins?" He stops a few feet away from me. "You actually think you can talk the cops out of locking this little 'terrorist' away?"

Jimmy takes another step up the ladder.

I'm not sure what bugs me the most, but something about the way the Chair's dealing with this news sets my ears on fire. "Yeah, that's exactly it," I say, not because I believe it, necessarily, but because I feel like saying something. I look at Jimmy, whose hard face has softened into a baby's, there, against the yellow boxes—like he's posing for a school photo. "It's better this way, Jimmy," I say. "Trust me. We're all going in, right after school tomorrow. My dad's picking us up—"

"Ha!" The Chair's laugh explodes like a firecracker as he walks away, yanking his spreadsheets out of the shoebox wall. Chuckling to himself and flipping the pages, he retreats to the back of the stockroom, where he leans against the door to the cruddy little employee bathroom. "Now I get it. This was your old man's idea."

I don't say anything.

The Chair snorts out another laugh. "In the land of the blind, the one-eyed man is king." He stares me down. "Have you thought about the punishment? Because there's definitely going to be punishment—"

"Yes. I know. But it'd be a lot worse, I bet, if they caught us themselves."

150

The Chair pauses, and it's difficult to read his expression. All I know is there's some weird tension in the stale stockroom air. I can feel it as he paces back up the aisle toward me. "This business of selling shoes," he says, glaring at me as he passes, "it takes a toll on a person."

"I bet it does."

"I mean, you hit a wall every now and then." The Chair turns at the top of the aisle and comes back down toward me. "You go numb. People pile it on and pile it on, but you just take it. You take it because you have to. And then one day you wake up very unhappy that you have to take it. You understand, maybe for the first time, what the *service* part of *customer service* means—to serve, *serv*ile, sub*serv*ient. And you wonder why you ever got into the business to begin with."

He leans on the wall directly across from me, wedging the spreadsheets in the stacks again. "And on that day, that bad day you stop fooling yourself, you wonder how you're ever going to face another customer. Ever. That was the kind of day I was having, Mitch, when you hit that Ginger."

"A historic event, looking back."

"Historic, indeed." He shoots me a hateful stare. "But now you want to unravel it all. And that, frankly, presents a problem. You go down to the police station, and what you've been doing gets connected back to me."

"I want the chaos out in the parking lot to stop. I want to surrender before they catch us—"

"And what about me?"

I hesitate. "What about you?" I look up at Jimmy, but

151

as soon as our eyes meet, he looks down at the floor. "We're not going to rat you out, Chair," I add, "if that's what you're worried—"

"No, you're definitely not," the Chair says, leaning away from the shoebox wall and poking me in the chest. "Because you're not going to the cops. We're all going to wait until this blows over. Isn't that right, Jimmy?"

The way the Chair looks at Jimmy then, smirking as Jimmy stares more intently at the floor, gets my blood pumping. "What, Chair, you don't trust us?" I say.

"Trust is not a value in my business. If it were, you wouldn't need a sales receipt. No. The answer is no. We wait."

The Chair and I stare at each other for what seems like an hour, each second filling the stockroom with gaseous stress. I can practically smell it.

"What's the deal, Chair?" I say. "Why are you being such a jerk?"

Before he can respond, Jimmy climbs down the ladder, steps between the Chair and me, and walks to the stock-room door.

"Where are you going, Jimmy?" I say.

He doesn't answer right away. He opens the door a crack and peers into the lot. "I'm through making trouble for everyone," he finally says, his back still to me.

"Well, it's a little late for that, don't you think, Biggins?" the Chair says, following him. "I mean, you mugged that old guy out in the parking lot. That's pretty serious."

Jimmy whirls around to the Chair, who's just a few feet

behind him now. A second later, though, Jimmy gazes past him and down the aisle at me.

That old tingle wraps itself around my neck. "Jimmy," I say, "that was a mistake. You can tell the cops you're sorry and offer to make rest . . . resti . . ."

"You're going to have a hard time catching a break from the cops if you don't even know how to say the damn word," the Chair says with a laugh.

Jimmy shifts his focus back to the Chair, his eyes narrowing, and then he turns around and continues scanning the parking lot. "What difference would an apology make?" he says, more or less to himself. "I've made plenty of those before. Nobody ever listened then, and they won't listen now." He speaks in that flat, emotionless voice I remember from the morning out by the kickboard, when he blew off Decker and left school.

"Jimmy, let's think about this for a second," I say.

He turns around again. "Chair says that if I go to the cops, he'll tell them I confessed to him about the Valley Road guy."

"What?" I look at the Chair, but he's shooting flamethrowers at Jimmy with his eyes. I turn back to Jimmy, whose expression is absolutely blank. "But you said that you weren't involved in that—"

"I wasn't," he says. "What I told you about that *is* totally true." He shrugs. "But, like I said, at this point I don't think it matters." He gives me one last classic Jimmy Biggins chin flip. "See you 'round, buddy."

When he turns his back to us again and slides his torso into the open sliver of door, the Chair walks up and leans

153

so he's speaking right in his ear. "Last chance, Biggins," he hisses. "It's my word against yours."

When Jimmy shoves open the stockroom door, Stu is standing right there. "Everything okay in here?" Stu says. "I heard some noise—hey! It's you!" Stu aims a meaty finger at Jimmy, then lunges for him.

Without a flicker of hesitation, Jimmy bulldozes Stu into the stockroom door and blasts out into the parking lot. He turns and waves for me to join him, then cuts a hard right for the river.

The Chair grabs my arm, but I knock his hand away, sending him back into the shoebox wall. Before Stu can regain his footing, I fly through the stockroom door. "Mitch Grant," Stu growls as he struggles to get up from the sidewalk.

A police car zips by, so close on Jimmy's heels it almost runs both of us over. I cut left and sprint in the other direction.

"I've got your number, Grant!" Stu shouts as I bolt across the near-empty lot.

A cruiser with its lights on turns into the mall entrance.

I head for the weeds separating the mall and the bank— an escape hatch I've used before.

I dash straight across Winston and plunge into the greasy secret world behind the fast-food joints that make Shunpike Falls what it is: a place you'd want to get in and out of as quickly as possible.

But what's my hurry? I've suddenly got nowhere to run. Like Stu said, they've got my number.

"Hey, Mitch," someone says as I pass in front of a Burger King dumpster.

My heart nearly jumps out onto the sticky pavement. I turn to find a kid from my school whose name I don't remember, sitting on a stack of empty bun racks, smoking a cigarette and talking on a cell phone. "You'll never guess who I just saw," he says into the receiver.

"Hey," I say, stopping in my tracks. I turn to the kid. "Do you think I could use your cell? It'll be quick. And it's local—Quarry."

19

Page and Marcus are dead silent in the jump seat of Dad's truck the whole way to the police station. I can't blame them. This situation wasn't supposed to go down until tomorrow, but if we want to turn ourselves in before we get caught, we don't have a second to spare. Stu sounded pretty serious when I blew by him in the ShUSA stockroom doorway.

I just hope that in this silent truck someone's doing some quality thinking—better, at least, than anything I've come up with so far. I mean, the plan was to have Jimmy in here with us. Obviously, the plan has changed. He's got to be long gone by now.

When we get to the Shunpike Falls Police Department, a stocky man with a ruddy face and a patch of snow-white hair, looking more like a social studies teacher than a cop, greets us in the lobby. "I'm Captain Freynne," he says, one hand in the pocket of his brown tweed jacket, the other holding a Styrofoam cup. "Is there something I can do for you?"

Dad steps up and shakes his hand. "I'm Reggie Grant."

Freynne pauses, squints, and takes a sip from the cup.

"Ah, yes," he says, wiping his mouth with his jacket sleeve. "The mall—"

"That's right. But it was a peaceful protest—"

"Oh, I remember, I remember."

"No harm done."

"No. You were well within your rights."

Dad looks down at his shoes. "For all the good it did me."

There's a long silence as all eyes turn to me. "I'm Mitch Grant," I say, stepping forward. "I'm here about the mall too."

Freynne gives me a somber look. "The more recent trouble with the mall, I take it."

"That's right, sir."

"I'm also involved," Page says and nudges Marcus.

"Me too," Marcus says.

Freynne folds his arms across his chest and doesn't say anything right away. "Dawson, we'll be in room C," he says to someone behind an information counter and gestures to a room off the lobby with a square glass window in the door. "Let's go in here."

The room isn't as bad as I imagined it'd be—certainly nothing like those interrogation rooms on TV cop shows. The table is just like the cafeteria tables at school, in fact, but without any graffiti scratched into it. There's a pitcher of water and some plastic cups, which Freynne begins filling when we're all seated.

"So, Mitch," he says as he sets a cup in front of each of us, "are you the one who can tell me how this all got started?"

"Well, sir," I say, "yes, I guess I'm the one who was most responsible—"

"We're all responsible," Page cuts me off.

Freynne arches a bushy eyebrow at her.

"Sorry," she says. "It's just . . ."

"No. No need to be sorry." Freynne holds up an empty cup. "Water?"

"Please." Page looks at me apologetically.

"I just meant," I begin again, "that, well, in the beginning it was just me. One night in early October."

"One night in early October," Freynne repeats and takes a pen from his jacket pocket. "What happened that night?"

I down my water. "Well . . ." I reach for the pitcher and pull it toward me. ". . . I'm not quite sure we're there yet."

Freynne gives me a puzzled look. "What do you mean?"

"What I mean is . . ." I pour another cup of water. ". . . you and I have to negotiate a little first." As I gulp away, I glance at Marcus, Page, and my dad. They all wear their own unique "What the hell are you trying to pull?" expressions.

"Negotiate?" Freynne says, giving Dad a look as if to see if he might clarify matters.

"That's right," I say before Dad can even open his mouth. *Negotiate.* The Chair's voice drifts into the room like the sound of Mom's television filtering down the hallway to my bedroom desk:

"In life . . . you don't get what you deserve. You get what you negotiate for."

158

"Explain to me just what we're negotiating," Freynne says, the slightest edge in his voice.

"Jimmy Biggins."

Freynne stares me down, but I don't turn away, mainly because I'd rather look him in the eye than see the "Don't go there" look my father is probably shooting me with every muscle in his face.

"What I think Mitch really means to say," Dad says firmly, "is that he'd like very much to tell you about his role in this mall trouble—"

"What I *mean* to say," I interrupt, "is this: I can tell you how this mall problem got started, but none of that will matter unless you clear Jimmy's name."

Freynne leans back in his chair, crosses his arms, and stares me down. "You know who pays my salary, don't you, Mitch?"

I nod.

"Well, the tax-paying citizens of Shunpike Falls expect a solution to this conflict that they can live with. And what I don't think you understand is that accountability needs to be a very large part of that solution."

"And what I don't think you understand, Captain Freynne," I say in a voice much sharper than I'd intended, "is that I'm not making demands. I'm telling you what *has* to happen."

Freynne leans forward and looks me squarely in the eye. "Let's just run a few numbers before we get too far off course here," he says. "Now, we're here to talk about the mall, right?"

I nod again.

"Well, technically, the harassment going on up there right now is a type of assault." Freynne pauses, one bushy eyebrow raised out of alignment with the other, as if giving me a minute to really think about what I've done. I'm familiar with this look from my many trips to elementary and junior high school principals' offices over the years, but Freynne uses it much more effectively than anyone I've ever met. "I wasn't sure if you were aware of that," he adds, "but, then, ignorance of the law is no excuse. So, yes, technically—assault." He pauses again—most effectively indeed. "So, now, let's get to the *other* type of assault tied in with all this. An assault by Jimmy Biggins? Do you know anything about that, Mitch? We had a report from a man who said he'd been physically assaulted in the mall parking lot."

I don't say anything. Out of the corner of my eye I can see Dad watching me, but I don't elaborate on the parking lot incident. The way I see it, I'm here to take responsibility for my own actions, not rat anybody else out for theirs.

Freynne's eyes don't move a millimeter from mine. "And there was, of course, an earlier assault up on Valley—"

"Jimmy had nothing to do with that," I snap. "You've got to understand, Captain Freynne, that Jimmy hasn't had many breaks."

"I understand, Mitch. But you know, physical assaults like these are quite different from the harassment I think you and your friends came in here to discuss. And Jimmy Biggins is a suspect in the other incident—"

160

"And I'm telling you, he's not the Valley Road guy—or guys."

"What makes you so certain? Do you know who is the Valley Road guy . . . or *guys?*"

I look back and forth between Page and Marcus as I weigh my options. Their eyes widen at the same time, revealing their surprise that I might actually know what happened on Valley Road. We don't keep many secrets from one another, the three of us, but I'm glad I've kept this one. What they don't know can't hurt them, like it could end up hurting me if I decide to take this conversation to a certain place and time.

"It's important that you say so if you do," Freynne goes on, "because the community is eager to see that crime solved—"

"The community," I interrupt, not really meaning to. "The community's got nothing to be afraid of."

"Well, that's not exactly how people feel these days. It's surely not what the shoppers up at the mall are feeling right now. They think the mall could be a target—"

"They think they have the first fricking idea about anything," I snap, again not really in control of my own words. "That's their biggest mistake."

An uncomfortable silence fills the room. Dad shifts in his chair, then pours a cup of water.

"I think I know what you're saying, Mitch," Freynne says and gives me a look that suggests he's not angry at my being so blunt with him—not yet anyway. "The question, I guess, is what do we do about it? How do we bring this all to a close?"

"No, not *how*," I say. "Who."

"Let me guess." Freynne tosses his pen down—the first clear sign of frustration I've seen from him since we've been sitting here. "Jimmy Biggins."

"Well," I add, trying not to sound too snotty, "he *is* the symbol of the whole thing."

"Symbol?" Freynne leans onto the table, picking his pen back up and tapping it on his notepad.

"Something like that," I say just as my stomach grumbles like a surly pitbull. "The kids who've been running wild through the mall parking lot over the past couple weeks got that bright idea after Jimmy's picture appeared in the *Beacon*. He's become a martyr, a hero."

Freynne stands up, squints at me for a few seconds, then, with a chuckle to himself, wanders over to the door and gazes out the window into the lobby. "That's absolutely fascinating." He turns to me. "He's a hero because the *Beacon* singled him out for giving shoppers a piece of his mind?"

I shrug. "I'm not saying it's logical. But, trust me, a lot of those mall shoppers aren't that nice."

Freynne returns to the table and rests one foot on his chair. "So, you three were all involved in this early on," he says, sounding as if he's still having some difficulty following the story. "Is that what I'm getting?" He turns to Marcus.

"That's correct, sir," Marcus says.

"So, why doesn't one of you tell the other kids to stop what they're doing up there?" Freynne stays focused on Marcus.

"They don't listen to us," Marcus says. "We were

popular for a little while, but we never had any control over anything. I mean, nobody actually cares what we *think*. For one thing, I'm black. And Page is the biggest femi-nazi in the whole school—"

"Hey," Page snipes back.

"I mean, in a good way," Marcus quickly adds.

Freynne looks toward the door again. "So Jimmy really is, as you say, the symbolic leader of the whole crusade?"

"To call it a crusade is a bit much," Page says. "I mean, it's not as if any of this was planned in any serious way."

Freynne nods a few times. "I'm glad to hear you say that. That's helpful—to your case, that is." He sits back down. "Still, what do we do about Jimmy?"

"It seems pretty straightforward to me," I say. "We clear his name, wipe his slate clean, and give Mrs. Pegg a call down at the *Beacon*."

Freynne looks at me, but his expression gives nothing away. I think I'm developing a sense of this guy, and I sense that he's not buying my proposal. "We're in a tough situation, Mitch," he says. That faint edge has returned to his voice. "The people of this community . . ."

I groan under my breath.

Freynne cocks an eyebrow at me. "What they want is to know where Jimmy Biggins is, what he's doing."

I give it one more try: "If you clear his name, maybe he'll come forward."

Freynne shakes his head. "Can't do it."

"Why can't you do it?"

"Come on, Mitch. We've already discussed it. Besides, in case you didn't know, your friend assaulted a security officer not an hour ago."

163

"That's not true," I say, although, the instant I say it, I realize that I should keep quiet about what I was doing and where I was about an hour ago. I can also see, from Freynne's perspective, that shoving Stu out of the way might technically *also* be a type of assault. The fact that Freynne doesn't mention the Chair, though, suggests that maybe the Chair and I are already involved in some wordless negotiations. I mean, if what Jimmy did to Stu was assault, what about my shoving the Chair out of the way? And if the Chair was going to tell Freynne that Jimmy confessed to Valley Road, why hasn't Freynne brought that up yet?

"Jimmy's kind of racking up points here," Freynne adds.

"Points," I mutter across the table. "You know who holds the *real* high score, don't you? Jimmy's parents."

"Mitch," Dad cuts in, "we're trying to be reasonable here—"

"Reasonable," I mutter again. "There's nothing reasonable about the way they treat him, and you know that." I don't look directly at Dad, who, I'm sure, is trying to give me a "Would you just chill out?" look. No way.

No one says anything. After a while, Freynne stands and walks to the door again. For a second, I think he's about to leave the room, but instead he turns and leans against the wall. "I'll tell you what, Mitch," he says, arms crossed, one hand still holding a cup. He seems to be studying me. "Here's what I can do. You tell me what your involvement in all this has been, and I can cut you a deal. The juvenile court and I'll work it out. You'll have to do some community service. Actually, you might have to do a lot of it."

Page and Marcus both exhale as though they've been holding their breath since entering the room.

"What about Jimmy?" I say. "No Jimmy, no deal—"

"Hold on, Mitch. Hear me out. Now, if Jimmy Biggins should present himself and confess to what he's done—and help us figure out what he hasn't done—well, we'll take things from there."

"You mean you'll send him to Cedarbrook."

Freynne holds his arms out to his sides in a helpless gesture I really don't like. "The judge will have to review Jimmy's case separately. There's no other way. But I can assure you maximum allowable leniency in proportion to his cooperation with our current investigation into Valley Road."

"You don't know Jimmy Biggins."

Freynne sighs. "Frankly, the Cedarbrook was built for a reason."

"He'll never get any better there."

"I'm afraid that's not for you to decide. But you can help him by encouraging him to come in on his own. That'll make a difference in how things turn out for him, I'm sure." At this, Freynne's expression looks almost sad, as if he'd offer us a better deal if he could.

I don't think Jimmy's ever coming in here. For that matter, I doubt I'll ever see that kid again. I haven't seen Jimmy Biggins *the kid* in a long, long time.

Still, what other option do I have but to trust this guy? I look at Page, Marcus, and Dad. They seem anxious, as if I might just blow the whole deal at any second.

"One night in early October," I begin again.

"Yes." Freynne eyes his pen on the table and returns to his seat.

"There was this woman . . ."

I tell the whole story, starting with the Ginger and ending with my rendezvous with Dad at the steak house. I leave out the names of the mall salespeople, although I'm tempted to rat the Chair out majorly. But I don't. I figure that if I leave him out of this, maybe he won't carry out his threat to set Jimmy up for Valley Road. What a slime bucket that guy turned out to be—never mind the suits, the nice shoes, and all that cheesy "looking for something in particular?" crap.

Valley Road. Although the words have nothing to do with me, Page, Marcus, Dad, or probably even Jimmy, they hang in the room like bad breath when I'm finished spilling my guts to Freynne.

"Is that more or less your understanding of things?" he asks Page and Marcus.

They both nod.

"Now can I speak to you privately?" I say before I really even know why I'd want to do such a thing.

Freynne shoots Dad a confused glance. "Uh, I don't see why not," he says. "Mr. Grant? Is that okay with you?"

Dad's now the one who seems to be having trouble following what's going on. "Uh, sure," he says. "Absolutely." He gives me a look only slightly less bewildered than the one he gave me when I first told him I was connected to all this madness.

"Well, if you'll excuse us," Freynne says, opening the door for the others, "Mitch and I'll just be a few more minutes."

When the door closes, Freynne sits back down across from me, leaning back more casually in his chair, as if he thinks I really just want to chat, you know, maybe talk a little football. "What's on your mind, Mitch?" he says.

To be honest, I'm not really sure—that is, I'm sure what's on my mind, but I'm still not sure what I want to tell this guy. I take a deep breath and try to block one particularly distressing set of images flashing in my mind: Randy Martello pinning me to the busted picnic table beneath the Legion Park rain shelter while Kirby Ploof draws a fist back again and again, one letter of my name tattooed on each knuckle.

"You had something you wanted to say to me?" Freynne continues, trying to be mellow but letting me know, in that way of his, that he doesn't really have all day to deal with a problem that could've been avoided if one kid from the Airport knew how to keep his smart mouth shut. "Maybe something about . . . Valley Road?"

I can't do it. I try to start telling him what I know, but the words won't come, even though I know everything would be so much better for Jimmy if they would. Oddly enough, Jimmy's just the thing that keeps me from ratting out Martello and Ploof: He'd hate for me to do it, to put myself in danger, for him.

"It's about Jimmy's parents," I finally say.

"Yes? What about them?" Freynne sits up straighter and reaches for his pen on the table.

I know I didn't come down here to rat anyone out, but I can't help telling this guy everything I know about life at the Biggins home, if you can call it life, if you can call it a home. Freynne writes a lot of it down, which gives me some hope that maybe someday someone will do something about Jimmy's parents. Of course, that could be as likely as a visit from the Tooth Fairy, but at the very least, as Page once suggested to Marcus, there'll be a record of the complaint somewhere.

Somewhere other than in Jimmy's scars.

～

As I step back into the lobby, where Page, Marcus, and Dad are waiting, the looks on their faces seem more fitting for someone coming out of major surgery. "I'm proud of you, Mitch," Dad says as we head for the door. "I'm sure your mother will be proud of you too."

The second he mentions Mom, her unmistakable, noisy VW pulls into the station lot. "Did Mom tell you she was coming down?" I say as I follow Dad out into the evening, which has grown pitch black while we were inside. I check my watch: eleven o'clock. Page and Marcus are probably out way later than they should be. For once, I bet that's not going to seem like such a big deal to their parents. Not when they hear where their kids have been.

"I never reached her," Dad says. "I left a message."

Mom steps out of the car and leans against the passenger door as we approach. She crosses her arms, as if she's mighty pissed about something, which she may very well be. I can't say that I haven't given her any reason. I mean, would she be here if I were such a little angel? "So, how'd everything go?" she says when I'm still about five yards away.

"Fine," I say. "We're going to have to do a bunch of community service."

"Consider yourselves damn lucky," she zings back. "And what about Jimmy?"

It's a strange question for Mom to ask, given that the last time his name came up in conversation between us she told me I had to stop being his friend.

"That's still undecided," I say. "The officer we spoke to, Captain Freynne . . ." I'm distracted by Mom wincing the right side of her face, as if she's suddenly developed a nervous tic I don't know about. "He said that . . ." She winces again.

"Mitch," Page says, just above a whisper.

When I look at her, she nods quickly in the direction of the VW's back seat.

"Don't be too obvious," Mom says in a voice no louder than Page's.

I glance in the back seat of Mom's car and see Jimmy's black boots. He's lying down on the floor. "What the . . ."

"He came by looking for you," Mom says, still whispering. "But you never came home. So, when he saw me pull in, he told me what happened, you know, at the mall. He told me a lot, actually." Mom takes a deep breath and glances once, lightning quick, at her car. "He asked me what he should do. I brought him inside, and we heard your father's message. Here we are. So, tell me, what do *you* think he should do?"

169

I just stare at my mother, not knowing what to say. I turn to Dad, but he seems in shock.

"Do it, Jimmy," Marcus says, though he says it to Page, giving her a little nudge in the shoulder to complete the effect that it's her he's talking to. "Show them who you really are."

"What will they do to me, Mitch?" Jimmy says from down below the window. "Are they going to send me to Cedarbrook?"

I focus on my mother, not wanting to alert anyone watching from inside the police station that I'm carrying on a conversation with an empty back seat. "They might," I say. "But it's Valley Road they're worried about, and you can deal with that." I've just oversimplified one of the most complicated matters in Jimmy's life—whether or not to rat out two dangerous guys, guys who happen to be his older brother's friends—but, deep down, I believe he should confess.

"And if you need a lawyer, Jimmy," Marcus says to Page with a totally false smile, "my folks will help you out. Promise."

"Mitch?" Jimmy says in a voice so scared-sounding, I'm glad I can't see him. "You're sure this is the right thing to do?"

I take one last look at my friends, my father, and Mom, who, surprisingly enough, is smiling at me ever so slightly. "I am," I say. "And whatever happens, I'll stick by you, man."

"We'll all stick by you," Page says, looking at me.

It's the first nice thing I've ever heard her say to him.

The back door pops open a second later, and we all step

170

back, as if we've just heard an explosion. "My neck is fricking killing me," Jimmy says as he spills out onto the pavement.

"You might want to watch the language," Dad says, helping him up.

"Everything Must Go!"

20

As cheesy as it may sound, I often look forward to the post–Thanksgiving dinner ritual of doing something with my parents: playing a board game, watching old home videos, going for a drive. Dad isn't much of a football fan, and both he and Mom are too naturally amped up to take naps in the middle of a perfectly good day, especially a day off from work.

This Thanksgiving's different, though, finding our household not exactly blanketed by a feeling of unity. My parents are civil to each other through the meal, which features an excellent turkey, just like always, but Dad's big news—that he's going to work for a real estate management company in another part of the state—sets a different tone for the day than in years past. Someone read about him in the *Beacon* and decided to give him a break. Only problem is, it's in a town about four hours' drive from Shunpike Falls. So he's moving.

Mom congratulates Dad when he tells us about the job, but she's very quiet for the rest of the meal. I don't know what she thinks about it all, but I have a feeling she's thinking about me, mainly, and what it's going to be like for me without a father around. I figure this has something to do with her deciding not to join us on a short drive around town after Dad and I finish the dishes.

Climbing into Dad's truck, I have to toss about a dozen copies of the *Beacon* into the jump seat so there's room to sit down up front. "Oh, yeah, those," Dad chuckles to himself. "Souvenirs, I guess."

As he pulls out of Mom's driveway, I take a copy of the paper from a smaller stack on the floor and read the headline. It's not news to me, but I read it again anyway:

House Painter Halts Mall Violence

When I first saw the paper a couple weeks ago, I was a little mad. I mean, while I was glad to see Dad's name presented in a positive light for a change, I couldn't really understand why Mrs. Pegg had taken what was essentially the story of a bunch of Shunpike Falls teenagers and turned it into one adult's story. Maybe she figured she owed Dad something for being the only person on her side back when the mall was still just a plan. Or maybe there's some unwritten journalism rule that whenever you write about teenagers, it's got to be bad news, but adults should be the focus of all good news.

Whatever the case, after the article came out, the youth of Shunpike Falls got behind Jimmy Biggins again and quit harassing shoppers at the Onion River Mall. After my first reading, I was nervous that nothing would change. I mean, Mrs. Pegg waited till the middle of the article to quote Jimmy. As Dad pulls onto Winston, I reread that section:

175

"I'm real sorry about the whole thing," Biggins said. "It was wicked stupid, it didn't accomplish anything good, and if I could take back everything I said and did, I totally would."

Even worse, Mrs. Pegg waited till the absolute very last paragraph to mention Jimmy's innocence in the Valley Road assault.

> While it has been confirmed that Biggins was not involved in the October assault of an elderly man on Valley Road, he may be tried in juvenile court for assaulting a Quarry man and a mall security officer in separate incidents at the Onion River Mall.

I'm still not sure if Jimmy had to tell Freynne who mugged that old guy on Valley Road or if he just had to prove that he didn't do it. I haven't seen much of Jimmy over the past couple of weeks. On Friday, I invited him over for Thanksgiving, but he said he had other plans. Maybe he ratted out Randy and Kirby, and now he's lying low. Like I said, I don't know. Page thinks that maybe Jimmy figures he's going to Cedarbrook and doesn't want to be reminded of how much more fun it is just hanging out with his friends in town, not that it's that great. I mean, even our mall turned out to be more trouble than it's worth. Still, I suppose it's better than juvie.

Adding to the rather gloomy quality of the day is the fact that there isn't a soul on the streets, not even a cable truck. Dad drives over the Onion River Bridge into

Queensbury and pulls a U-turn right in the middle of the road. He drives midway back across the span and pulls over so that we're facing Shunpike Falls. We get out of the truck and walk to the railing, where we look out over the river for a while without saying anything.

The Onion rumbles like some huge, noisy machine as it pumps on, dark as a winter night. I follow the crystal-tinged weeds that lean into the water from the edge of the meadow on the far bank and gaze back into the smooth knolls of Queensbury. The morning's dusting of snow still clings to tree branches and old houses over there, making the town look like it exists in another time, maybe a hundred years ago. I imagine the Queensburians sitting in big leather chairs around cozy, fire-lit rooms, eating cheese and crackers, smiling contentedly. I try to imagine what that feels like: a fireplace, cheese and crackers, no worries.

A stiff wind kicks up, driving the slate-gray river like a herd of angry cattle, slipping up over the bridge railing to wrap my jacket around my body, as if to turn me away from Queensbury, tucked like a baby into the hills. The town's well-placed trees rattle their skeletal branches. *Shoo!*

My eye is drawn back to the little clearing in the weeds on the Shunpike Falls side of the river where I spotted Jimmy a few weeks ago. The jagged piece of plastic he used to shield the wind has blown downriver a few yards, where it sits balled up. I follow a path through brush and dead trees, past some mangled shopping carts, and into the back parking lot of the mall. "*Caveat emptor,*" I say, more or less to myself.

Dad puts an arm around me. "Yeah. You can say that

again. Here, I want you to check something out." He points with his other arm beyond the nearly empty mall parking lot. "Can you see Mo's Hots?"

"Yeah."

"Well, you see . . . you can just barely see it from here . . . but there's a clearing behind Mo's that extends back about five acres."

"Right, I see it."

"Well, imagine a big circle another five acres across. And it reaches from Mo's to that clearing, then up to the McDonald's drive-thru lot to the east, then back down here to . . . what's that place there—"

"Taco Bell—"

"That's the new one, right?"

"Relatively."

"Well, that place wasn't there when these plans were drawn up." He walks a few steps toward town and leans on the guardrail. After a minute or so, he raps his knuckles on the railing and turns to me. "It would've worked," he says with certainty. "It absolutely would've worked. Come here."

I walk to his side.

"You see how Route Four cuts away from the river, here, and funnels into this fork at the Winston and Riverside intersection?"

"Right. You can see the mall off to the right as you're coming down Route Four—"

"Exactly. Only, Winston Road would've worked just as well as an entrance to Shunpike Common. You see, if people don't cut off Riverside toward the mall, they head straight for . . . what?"

"McDonald's."

"Sure. Off to the left. Can't miss it, right? You can see those godawful golden arches from a mile up Route Four. So, just for the sake of argument, let's say there is no mall. So, you're driving down Route Four, and you see the golden arches, and you wheel on over there. But imagine that just as you get there—or maybe you're already inside McDonald's—and you look out the window toward Mo's and you see this quaint little green, you know, with a gazebo and everything."

"Where, behind Mo's? Like, where all those dumpsters—"

"Mo was with us on this. He was going to sell his lot in exchange for a new restaurant in a section of the ring."

"The ring?"

"The ring of shops that would've run in a little, kind of arcing strip—a very tastefully designed strip—of shops around the east arc at the top of the circle there. We would've had Mo's lot to seed over, maybe put in picnic tables. There was even talk about a public pool."

"A pool?" The idea seems like pure fantasy. To me and a lot of other kids from the Airport neighborhood, a pool is something a person hops in and out of late at night in someone else's yard. Then you run like hell.

"Yeah. A municipal pool. Crazy, huh?"

As we gaze out over Shunpike Falls, for once I can actually see what my father has been rambling on about all these years.

"Would've been a nice place to get together, interact with one another," he says. "This . . . this sprawl would've had some center to it, some method to the madness."

"That's pretty cool, Dad."

"Not bad for a house painter, right?" He shakes his head, chuckles to himself, and sighs.

I stare upriver.

"The mall's going to take it on the chin this year, I can just feel it," Dad says more somberly. "And it's got nothing to do with all that . . . well, you know, the trouble. That Wal-Mart in Quarry is really cutting into mall business, just like I knew it would. Word is, Quarry may also get Home Depot in the spring. Businesses here in the Falls—all of them, not just in the mall—will have their work cut out for them. That'll bring people together for something, at least. Who knows, maybe they'll even come around on the Shunpike Common idea."

He kicks a pebble under the bridge railing and watches it fall down to the river. "Sometimes the best you can do is leave your plans lying around, Mitch, let people come to them in their own time. Because if there's one thing I've learned, it's that people are too stubborn to convince unless they're faced with some . . . crisis." After a long pause, he turns to me. "You going to be okay, son?"

"I'll be fine."

"You think you can handle this community service deal?"

"It's not that bad."

"Two hundred hours. Is that what they said?"

I nod. "I'll take it. Anyway, they said we could wait till Christmas break to get started. They've got Page and me out at Riverview Residences, doing kitchen work mostly, shoveling snow when it comes. If things go well, they